# HEART SCARS

**PALMETTO**
PUBLISHING
Charleston, SC
www.PalmettoPublishing.com

© 2024 by Colleen Gaderick

All rights reserved.
This book or any portion thereof may not be reproduced or used in any manner whatsoever without the express written permission of the publisher except for the use of brief quotations in a book review.

Paperback ISBN: 9798822966055
eBook ISBN: 9798822966062

# HEART SCARS

COLLEEN GADERICK

# CHAPTER 1
# 2023

"Which one should we get? The spinach, or the cheese, or the lobster? Maybe we should just get all three."

I hear him, but I'm not really listening. This is our typical trip to the organic food market. I already said that I thought we had enough ravioli in the freezer at home, but Noah thinks that we should buy more. We always end up buying a lot more things than we really need. The conversations always go this way, and, as always, he will win.

I love him. He's a good man, but sometimes he really frustrates me, and I'm becoming more and more aware that something is missing in our marriage. There's a void, and I just don't feel 100 percent content, like I'm constantly restless. Noah works hard, and he cares about my happiness and well-being. He's everything I thought I ever wanted, really everything most women want. I should be deliriously happy, right? But something just feels *off*, like there's a piece missing.

I consider myself a realist, and I know that even the best relationships are a choice and take an enormous amount of hard work on both sides. But sometimes I'm also a hopeless romantic and I frequently scold myself, like I'm doing right now, for wanting too much. I have never, not even for one second, believed in that fairy-tale movie plot crap that you always see where the girl and the guy lock eyes and *magic* happens, so what happens next makes me question everything.

I'm lost in thought as I watch a girl pour samples of wine and set out an array of cheeses. I'm about ready to head over and try one or two of those wines when I look up and see him coming down the aisle—he's a really good-looking guy, but what has stopped me in my tracks is that his eyes are fixated on me. And, for some unknown reason, I can't look away.

After what seems like a very long time, I turn my attention back to the display of pasta in front of me and try to look like I'm intent on making a decision. The guy who was staring walks by me, and I can't explain it any other way except to say that I can feel it. I literally feel a jolt inside my body as he goes by. He bumps my arm with his basket as he is passing by, and I honestly believe it was an accident—it's Saturday and the small store is absolutely packed.

"Oh my gosh, I'm so sorry," he says.

"No worries," I reply and then turn back around to Noah, who was right beside me just a few seconds ago, but he has moved on to the cheese case, and I see that he isn't even looking in my direction.

The guy who bumped me is still right behind me, and he says, "It's really a zoo in here today." I steal a quick glance at Noah and see that he still hasn't even looked up, so I turn to face the unbelievably good-looking stranger.

"It sure is. I should know better than to come here on a Saturday."

"Me too," he says. "I usually come on Fridays around two o'clock. It's a lot less busy then." I want to stop looking at him, but I can't seem to turn away. He doesn't take his eyes off me either. We just keep looking at each other for several seconds, until I finally manage to find the power of speech again.

"Thanks, that's good to know." By this time I see that Noah is staring at me with a puzzled look on his face, so I just say, "Well, have a good day." He apologizes again for bumping my arm and tells me to have a good day too. I make my way up to where Noah is, and he asks me who I was talking to.

"Oh, I don't know. He accidentally bumped into me because it's so crowded in here, and he was just saying sorry."

"Oh," Noah responds and starts pushing the cart that now has six packages of pasta and four types of cheese in it.

I look back one more time and see that the stranger who bumped me is about to go around the corner, but right before he disappears, he gives me a big smile. I drop my head because I suddenly feel like I've done something wrong. I also become very aware of how I'm dressed, and it's not very good. I've got on sweatpants, an old tank top, and a baseball cap. Suddenly I wish I was dressed better and had put some effort into my hair, but I'm also confused as to why I'm thinking this way at all!

*** 

At home we unpack the groceries and try to find room in the freezer for more pasta that we didn't need. Noah goes outside to do some yard work, and I go about my day of vacuuming, doing laundry, and getting dinner ready, but I can't get my mind off of the man who bumped into me…

"Ridiculous!" I scold myself out loud.

After we finish dinner, Noah and I move over to the couch to watch television, which is our usual routine. We watch an episode of a show that we can both agree on, and Noah is snoring next to me by eight thirty.

# CHAPTER 2
# 2002

It's late August in 2002, and I'm eighteen. I live in Iowa, and, unlike a lot of days in Iowa, the weather is picture perfect outside—bright blue sky, sunshine, and eighty-two degrees.

I'm heading to the church because I'm about the get married. My mother, Lana, is ecstatic because she wants me to be just like her: dependent on a man, having children, and living in the same small town that I've grown up in for the rest of my life.

I'm a cliché. I'm much too young to understand the commitment and sacrifices it takes to make a successful marriage. Not to mention I'm about to marry the first and only boyfriend I've ever had. I didn't even start dating until I was seventeen, and Greg was one of the first guys I ever went out with. He's three years older than me and works as a cook at a local restaurant. He's a nice guy, but we don't have much in common, except that we both grew up poor and in the same small town. I'm not in love with him, and I'm sure he's not in love with me, but we convince ourselves that we are ready for marriage.

And at this moment, it sounds pretty good to me—I'm dying to get out of the tiny, dysfunctional home that I live in with my mother and alcoholic stepfather. I desperately want to go to college, but I get no help from my parents, and I'm too young and naïve to know how to make it happen on my own.

Greg and I stand at the altar and take our vows. As we walk out of the church, now husband and wife, I'm hoping that we will be happy and that I'll be able to build a life and a family with this man. Maybe we can have it all if we really work at it and we can grow to love each other. And maybe I can eventually go to college and have the children that Greg wants to start having right away. Not that I don't want to have kids, but I'd rather wait until I'm in my mid-twenties at least. Looking back now, I should have known that it would never work.

Being married at eighteen and twenty-one is harder than we ever dreamed it would be. We are living in a small suburb about fifteen miles outside of a large city in Iowa—we moved three hours away from our hometown for better jobs right after we got married. Most of the time we are broke and have to work long hours just to pay for the small apartment we live in. We are fighting constantly. He's unnecessarily jealous of the guys I work with, and I'm not happy. I just keep hoping that things will get better with time.

We both work hard, taking on double shifts whenever we can, and eventually go from our tiny apartment to a tiny house. He doesn't want me to work. He wants babies, lots of babies, and he wants them right now. I decide that I might change my mind about being such a young mom and agree to try to start a family. I really just want to stop fighting about it, and I know that it will make Greg happy. I agree to stop working because he convinces me that we will soon have little ones running around, and we both feel that I should be home to take care of them.

After I stop working, we sell my car and only have Greg's car now—the same one he's had since he was sixteen. Greg works second shift at a restaurant that is more than an hour from where we live, so I'm left alone in the house from about one thirty in the afternoon until he comes home at around midnight. I can't go anywhere because he has the car, and now I live hours away from all my friends. Months and months go by, and he grows increasingly irritated at the fact that I'm not pregnant yet. And I'm bored out of my mind. I want to go to college and go back to work. Greg insists that I hold off and just give it a little more time.

More than a year goes by, and I'm still not pregnant. We find out that I'm infertile and not likely to conceive on my own. Greg wants to talk about fertility drugs or adoption, but I'm not interested in those options. I'm firmly set on it happening naturally or not happening at all.

I decide that I'm going back to work and going to school. This does not sit well with Greg. I get a job that's just around the block from our house, so I'm able walk to work. Then I enroll in a couple of classes. I take the bus to college for the first few months, but then Greg gets a small raise and we buy a cheap second car. Since I'm finally able to go to college, I want to stop trying to get pregnant, and we start using birth control.

A little over three years into the marriage, we move back to our hometown because Greg gets an opportunity to work at a new restaurant that just opened. I get a job at a local medical center, working three days a week, and he starts working at the restaurant, his hours being mostly the day shift. I decide I want to keep going with my education and start taking classes to become a dental hygienist. It's going to take quite a while to complete because I'm only able to take classes two days a week, but I'm determined to finish. Greg keeps pushing me to start trying to have children again, but I tell him that I don't feel that the timing is right.

This is the first time that we've ever worked almost the same hours, and neither one of us knows what to do with all the time we have together. We never had much of anything in common, and it's more obvious than ever. I end up spending as much of my free time that I can with my best friend, and Greg goes out fishing or spends time with his brother every weekend. We start to spend very little time together and always end up fighting whenever we are together. He threatens me with divorce pretty often, and after four miserable years, I decide that splitting up would be the best option.

The divorce is very tough on me. I feel like a failure. Greg fights me every step of the way, even though he seemed to want the divorce just as much as I did. My mom takes Greg's side and pretty much cuts me out of her life. She has no problem telling me that the divorce was 100 percent my fault, that I'll never find another guy that will be as good to me as Greg was, that I should have given him the kids he wanted, and on and on. I finally tell her that as long as she continues to talk to me this way, I don't want to see her anymore. She tells me that's fine with her, and that begins a two-year stretch of her not speaking to me.

I feel like I couldn't get any lower.

# CHAPTER 3
# 2023

It's Friday around one o'clock, almost one week since I was bumped into at the market. Friday is my day off, since the dental office is closed then. It's my favorite day of the week—I get time to myself and can do whatever I want.

I try to distract myself by reorganizing my closet, but I keep thinking about going to the market…at about two o'clock. Even though I've tried to talk myself out of it, I'm pretty sure that I'm going to go. I convince myself that we do need a few groceries. I curl my hair, spend extra time on my makeup, and pick out a cute outfit to wear. I keep thinking that I shouldn't do this and I feel guilty, but I just can't deny the fact that something is compelling me to go.

I'm sitting in my car in the parking lot at exactly 1:50 p.m., debating if I should get out or not. Again, I reason with myself and conclude that I could stand to pick up a few things. I take a deep breath and get out of my car. I grab a cart and head inside.

He was right; the market is almost empty at this time. I start wandering up and down the aisles, and every once in a while, I glance around to see if I spot him. I shake my head, thinking to myself that this is really stupid. I should just get some bread and a salad and head home for my usual Friday night routine.

For a moment I'm truly preoccupied, trying to decide what type of bread I should get, when I hear a voice say, "So you took my advice, huh?"

I look up and wow! It's him. I let my eyes roam over him for a moment before I respond. He's got on a white T-shirt that fits like it was made for him; so do his jeans. He's clean shaven, and his hair looks effortlessly perfect. He has muscular arms, and he must spend a lot of time outside because he's quite tan. He's more handsome than I remembered from last week. I feel like there are butterflies in my stomach, my face feels warm, and I can tell that I'm blushing.

Shaking myself out of my stupor, I say, "Excuse me?"

He looks surprised and, I think, a little disappointed. I suddenly feel like I need to backtrack. I had been trying to sound casual, like I really didn't remember our brief encounter last weekend.

I follow up with a nod of my head. "Oh yeah, you were the one who told me this is a good time to shop here. Thanks for the tip." The disappointed look on his face is replaced by a smile. I look down at my cart and realize it's completely empty. I bite my lip. Hard. So stupid—it looks like I've been waiting for him. If he notices, his expression doesn't show it.

"I'm Jordan," he says, and I tell him my name's Kate. We start a casual conversation about how nice the weather is, how we hope it's going to be a good summer, that they're predicting more rain than usual. All I can think is, Where is this going? He has to know that I'm married because he saw me with Noah. There isn't a ring on his finger, but there's a pretty big one on mine.

"Are you picking up things for dinner for you and your husband tonight?" he asks, as if on cue. I cringe inside, mostly because I feel guilty for being here at all and partially because I don't want him to tell me to enjoy my day and walk away.

"Yes, probably. Yeah, I was just looking for a few things, I guess." As the words come out of my mouth, I'm dying inside. I sound like a babbling idiot.

He doesn't seem to notice and changes the subject. "The one thing that I hate about this store is that it's always so cold in here."

I'm wearing a sundress and look down to see that my legs that are covered in goosebumps. It seems strange to me because I don't feel cold at all right now. Then I tell him that I hate being cold. I'm reaching for anything that might keep us talking. He offers up that there's a coffee shop right next door.

"Would you like to go get a cup and warm up?" he asks.

I pause. I know that it's wrong but tell myself that having a cup of coffee in the middle of the day is no crime. "Sure, just let me pay for my groceries." I cringe again because this causes him to look down at my empty cart.

"Looks like you won't be spending a lot of money today." We both laugh. I tell him that I just got here and I need to get a couple of things. He says same for him, and we agree to meet at checkout. I make sure that everything I buy can sit in the car for a while. After checking out I put my groceries in the trunk of the car, and he does the same.

We walk over to the coffee shop side by side but in complete silence. There's a weird mix of guilt and excitement surrounding us. We walk in, and he steps ahead of me and immediately pulls a chair out for me to sit down. Such a small thing, but I love it. He asks me what I'd like. I tell him just a regular coffee is fine. I start to unzip my purse but he insists on paying for mine too. Before I can argue, he is already up at the counter.

I look around to see if I recognize anyone. The market is way out on the edge of town, and I'm pretty sure that anyone from my neighborhood probably wouldn't be here. Besides, I tell myself, how would any of them know that he isn't my brother-in-law or my cousin or something anyway? I sure am finding a lot of ways to reason with myself that there's nothing wrong with what I'm doing.

He comes back with our coffees and sits down across from me. I really take notice of his eyes for the first time. They are strikingly blue. I have blue eyes, but they are a dark blue. His eyes are the color of crystal-clear Caribbean water. We both realize that neither one of us is saying a word. Then we both start to laugh.

I shrug my shoulders, shake my head, sigh, and say, "What are we doing?"

"I have absolutely no idea."

I track his bright blue eyes as they move to my left hand, to my ring. "You know that I'm married."

"I know, and you're right, I don't know what we're doing here."

"I don't see a ring on your finger, so I assume you're not married." He looks sad for a moment and tells me that he's a widow. Out of pure instinct I tell him I'm so sorry, then reach out and grab his hand. This sounds like some typical bullshit, fairy-tale statement that I would laugh and roll my eyes at, but I actually feel a jolt of electricity run through my body. I pull my hand away quickly, before I can gauge his response, and look down at my coffee.

He offers, without my prodding, that his wife was killed in a car crash. He tells me that it happened more than eight years ago and that they had only been married a little over a year when it happened. My heart genuinely hurts for him.

"She was really amazing, and I still miss her every day. And right now I'm thinking that if I found out that she had coffee with some random guy, I would be very upset."

This is it, I think to myself. He's realizing, like I already did, that this is not right. I brace myself for him to scoot his chair back, say he's sorry, and walk away. But that doesn't happen.

"I wish I could explain it, but I can't. For some reason I just feel like I really need to talk to you. But there can't be anything else—all we're going to do is talk."

"Right, right, you are right." I think I just said right five thousand times. *Ugh!*

# CHAPTER 4
# 2006

I'm twenty-two and newly divorced. I'm living on my own for the first time, and I'm terrified. I've never been on my own. I went straight from my childhood home to being married. I'm not making very much money and still going to school when I can. I'm really worried that I won't be able to pay the rent, my car payment, and utilities and still be able to eat! I imagine having to call my mother, who turned her back on me, and tell her that I've failed.

Out of panic I take up with the first guy I start dating after my divorce. I met him in a nightclub right before my divorce was final. His name is Alex, and he's just relocated from a different state. He was in a relationship, but when it fell apart, he decided to come live with his brother in Iowa.

He's aggressive, drinks too much, and has no respect for women. Deep down, I know I'll come to regret it, but he wants to move into my apartment with me so that we can share expenses because he desperately wants to move out of his brother's house. Looking back, I know that the best thing I could have done is tough it out on my own, work two jobs if I had to, and learn how to live alone. But when you're young, it's so hard to see these things.

Our relationship is volatile from the beginning. He's verbally abusive, leaves me at home alone to go out drinking with his friends, and threatens to move out constantly. I'm still working at the local medical clinic as a front desk clerk and sometimes do additional clerical work at home on the weekends for extra money. We don't spend much time together, but eventually I just try to accept that, for now, this is the best I'm going to get. Young and stupid, for sure!

I continue pushing forward with the relationship. Sometimes we go out together, but it always ends up with him getting drunk and telling me he's going to leave me and go back to his ex-girlfriend. One night he's being his usual belligerent self, and I've had enough. I tell him he's a drunk loser and that I want him to move out. He suddenly shoves me. Hard. I wasn't expecting it, and I fall to the floor. He leaves me with a final "Fuck you, you stupid bitch!" I'm relieved when he storms out the door.

As it is with most abusers, Alex is full of apologies the next day. I don't say much and he goes into to damage control mode. He stops drinking, is sweeter to me than he's ever been, sends me flowers, gives me cards, cooks me dinner, and proclaims his eternal love for me. This goes on for a few months, and I truly believe he's changed, but it doesn't last long. Slowly I notice a change in his demeanor again. He becomes moody and quiet, and it doesn't take much to set him off. One day he just suddenly tells me that we aren't right for each other and that he's moving back in with his brother.

I should rejoice in the fact that he has given me my "out," but instead I'm lonely and I miss the "good version" of him that I had for the past couple of months. I decide that I have to move on, and I finally get to experience my twenties on my own. And I embrace it fully! I'm out with friends almost every weekend. We go shopping and go out dancing, and, for the first time, I'm just really enjoying myself.

I'm having a great time, but right when I think I've got a handle on being single, you guessed it, Alex resurfaces. I tell him that I won't see him again, but he starts the same pattern of the flowers, calls, letters, and cards. He swears he's changed and is so in love with me. It eventually wears me down, and we start having a relationship again, but I won't let him move back in to my apartment.

I get a small promotion at work and start making a little more money, but I'm still pursuing a career as a dental hygienist. I buy a house. It's tiny and needs some work, but it's all mine! Alex wants to move in with me. I'm hesitant, but things have been going well, so I decide to let him come back. He's gotten a really good job that involves travel, which is fine because between work and school, I'm not home a lot either. He likes his new job, and we are getting along great. I start to think that maybe he just needed to grow up a little and this just might work. Funny how you can make yourself forget all the bad stuff when things are going well.

It's Christmas, 2007. We unwrap presents, and when we're done, Alex tells me that there's another one for me and hands me a small box. I open it, and there's an engagement ring inside. I hesitate but say yes. I convince myself that everything is going to be great, and we start planning a wedding and our future together.

Again, the good times don't last long. Just a couple of months later, he pulls another disappearing act, this time telling me that he's still in love with his ex, she wants him back, and he's going to move back to Florida to be with her. I'm pretty devastated, but I have to accept the fact that he's leaving. This time I quickly move on with my life.

A couple months later, I get a call from Alex. He tells me that leaving me was a huge mistake and that as soon as he got to Florida, he knew he made the wrong decision and he wants to come home. I stick to my guns this time and tell him there's no way he can come back to *my* house.

He moves back to Iowa but gets his own apartment and his old job back. The same love-bombing pattern returns, and we talk every night on the phone before bed. He always ends the conversation by telling me that he still wants to marry me and that he's not giving up. He is slowly wearing me down. The next thing I know, we are engaged again and move forward with the wedding. To this day I still can't believe that I was sucked in again, and it's probably the biggest regret of my life.

I know that I shouldn't marry him—even as I'm walking down the aisle I feel the urge to run—but I go through with it. Looking back, I think because we had broken up and gotten back together so many times, I just couldn't face having to tell people that I was calling off the wedding. I know now that the temporary embarrassment would have been a million times better than what I ended up enduring.

The marriage is immediately up and down. The verbal abuse starts again just weeks after we marry, and it only escalates. Alex calls me a bitch and a whore and tells me I'm boring and ugly. One night, the verbal abuse turns physical again. I'll always remember it vividly because I experienced what it feels like to not know if you're going to be alive the next day. Scared to death is an understatement. The fight starts like they all do—he's unhappy, I'm not what he wants, I'm ugly, etc.

I finally tell him to just leave then, and he goes crazy. He's punching me in my arms, shaking me, and ultimately punches me in the face so hard he knocks me down. I sit on the floor stunned while he tears up things in the house. I see an opportunity to get away from him when he's ripping a door off the hinges. I grab my car keys, sneak out and leave. I know I should have gone straight to the police station and had him arrested, but, again, I think I didn't do it because I didn't want to face the public shame. Bad decision, and it's one I'll always regret.

I stay away for several hours, and when I come home, he's ironing his clothes and packing like nothing happened. I have my finger on a can of mace that I carry on my keychain, but no need to worry—he's perfectly calm, and you'd never know that he was violently attacking me four hours ago. As soon as

I walk in, he apologizes, swears it will never happen again, and promises that he is going to get some counseling.

But what he doesn't know is that I've made a decision. He's leaving the next day and will be working out of town for an entire week. I tell him that everything is fine, I forgive him, and I assure him that I'll be there when he gets home. He says he's tired and asks me if I'm ready for bed. I have no intention of sleeping in the same bed with him ever again. I tell him I'm not tired yet and that I'm going to read for a little while. I stay up as late as I can, until I'm certain he's asleep, and I sleep on the couch that night. After he leaves the next morning, I pack up all his things and take them to his brother's house. The day before he's due to come home, I call him and tell him he no longer lives with me; I've already moved all his things out of the house and filed for divorce. There's not much he can do about it, and he just has to accept it.

After less than one year of marriage, we are divorced.

I'm not upset at all to be away from him, but I feel embarrassed and defeated.

# CHAPTER 5
# 2023

My coffee cup has been empty for a while, and so has his. I keep wondering who is going to make the move to get up and leave first. But we just keep making small talk about our lives, our hobbies, and our jobs.

He's an investment banker and only works three days a week. He bought shares of some very successful stocks several years ago and made enough money for him to be able to afford to work less, even though he's only thirty-nine, his birthday being exactly two months before mine. He says that he decided to cut way back on work after his wife died. It gave him a new perspective on what's important in life, and work is definitely not his top priority anymore.

I can't help but compare him to Noah, and I know it's not fair. Noah works very hard and that has given us a comfortable lifestyle, but he's almost obsessed with work. He's constantly on his computer or phone. And when he's not, then he's talking about work.

I look at my watch and I'm shocked to see that we've been sitting here for almost three hours! I know that I should go, but I just can't make myself leave. Actually I have all night—Noah is traveling for work all weekend and won't be back until

Sunday night. He travels a lot for his job and is out of town at least one weekend a month.

I'm snapped out of my thoughts when he says, "Are you getting hungry?"

I didn't expect him to say that and contemplate how to respond for a few seconds. I lie and say, "No, not really." I instantly regret it because I'm pretty sure he wants to ask me to have dinner with him.

"Okay then, I guess I should get going."

I feel a twinge of disappointment. "Right, right, me too." I really wish I could stop saying right!

He walks me to my car, and we just stand there awkwardly. He's got his hands in his pockets and I'm fiddling with the strap of my purse. What am I supposed to say here? And besides that, what do I think is going to happen now? He finally ends the silence.

"Well, maybe I'll see you next Friday," he says a bit hopefully.

I try to sound nonchalant and say, "Yeah, well, maybe." For a second it looks like he's leaning in for a hug and then changes his mind.

He gives me a big smile and says, "Thanks for spending time with me. I really enjoyed your company, Kate."

"My pleasure, and thanks for the coffee, Jordan."

He walks away and I get in my car. I'm suddenly aware of my sweaty palms and the fact that I can literally hear my heart beating. What the hell?! I drive home feeling a mix of excitement, fear, and guilt. I literally go from feeling euphoric one minute to feeling sick the next. I pull into the garage and go into the house.

Almost as if on cue, my phone rings. It's Noah. He says he's just calling to check on me and see how my day went. I feel like the worst person on Earth. He asks what I did, and I quickly run down the list: worked out, cleaned, did laundry, and went to the market for a few things. I ask him how his trip is going, and he launches in to telling me every detail about his

19

flight, his hotel room, and what he had for dinner. Despite all his good traits, this is one of the things that I can barely tolerate—he hardly listens to what I've just said and sometimes doesn't even respond before he launches into telling me every little detail about his day.

After ten minutes he finally pauses and asks me what I had for dinner. I hesitate and look at the clock. It's after seven. I say that I got caught up in doing a little organizing in our closet and haven't eaten yet. I feel like I have to explain what I've been doing and start talking about getting a bag of clothes together to take to Goodwill and ask if there's anything he wants me to put in it for him. He obviously isn't listening because he doesn't respond to my question and starts, again, telling me every last detail of his day. I know that my life can be a little mundane, but would it kill him to say something, anything, when I talk?

Sometimes I feel like I'm living in a bubble and no one sees or hears me.

I go to bed early, but I definitely can't sleep. I can't stop thinking about where I was just a few hours ago. I feel like it's going to be agony not knowing how long it will be until I "accidentally" bump into him again. I repeat his name over and over again in my mind as I drift off to sleep: Jordan, Jordan, Jordan…

I have no idea that just a few miles from where I'm falling asleep in my bed, he is lying in his bed thinking: Kate, Kate, Kate…

***

I meet my best friend, Liz, for lunch the next day. We have been best friends since we were eleven. Her mom also worked in housekeeping at the hotel where my mom worked when I was a kid, and they introduced us. Liz, her sister Tracy, and I clicked from day one, and Liz and I have remained inseparable ever since. I still talk to Tracy, but she lives in Iowa so we don't see each other very much anymore.

I have decided not to tell Liz anything about yesterday. This further drives home the point to me that I feel guilty, because I tell her absolutely everything. We are like sisters, and there's really nothing about me that she doesn't know. But I just want to keep Jordan all to myself, and I'm pretty sure that she wouldn't approve of what I'm doing, which is fair because don't approve of what I'm doing. She's been married for seventeen years and, for the most part, has a happy marriage. They have a fifteen-year-old daughter and seem to have a good life together.

Liz and I do our usual today—lunch, shopping, and laughing together until our stomachs hurt. When she and I are together, it's truly nonstop fun. We hang out all afternoon and into the early evening.

When I get home, I get out the big box that I keep tucked away in the back of the closet and start looking at old photos and notes. Earlier in the day, Liz and I were reminiscing about a concert we went to when we were sixteen and she asked me if I still had the pictures from that day. I told her I was certain that I did, and I was sure they were somewhere in my "memories" box at home. Whenever I look through the box, it's a rollercoaster of emotions, so many good memories but some bad ones too. It's full of old pictures, ticket stubs, letters, and cards.

People ask me why I don't get rid of the things from my past relationships that ended so badly. I think that I keep them as a reminder of how far I've come since then. Now that I have a good man, I certainly don't want to mess it up, so why in the world can't I stop thinking about some guy I met at the grocery store?!

As I'm sifting through the box, I find a picture of the last serious boyfriend I had before I met Noah. Looking at it makes me sad and angry at the same time.

# CHAPTER 6
# 2011

I'm only twenty-seven and have been divorced for the second time for almost two years. I've spent my time working. A lot. And going to school. I finally finished the program and got my first job as a hygienist working in a small dental office. I'm making more money and enjoying life on my own.

To say I'm cautious about men now is an understatement. I've had a few dates but haven't really connected with anyone. One Friday night, I'm out with friends and meet a seemingly nice guy. His name is Vincent, and we hit it off immediately. It seems crazy to me how much we have in common—from movies to music and, especially, our sense of humor. I honestly feel like we are almost exactly alike, aside from the fact that he grew up in a wealthy family. But despite the money, his family is almost as dysfunctional as mine.

We start dating and are inseparable pretty quickly. This is the first relationship where I'm having a lot of fun. We are constantly taking trips, going to concerts, and generally just loving our life together. We live apart but stay with each other every weekend and at least one day a week.

After more than a year together, I'm growing restless. As great as our relationship is, he hasn't said I love you, and I'm getting tired of the thirty-plus-minute commute when we want to see each other.

It's Halloween, and we dress up in costumes and go to a party out of town. We have a few drinks and take a cab back to our hotel room. I've had more than a couple of drinks and feel brave enough to tell him that I love him. My proclamation is met with silence.

"Well, that's not the response I was hoping for," I say.

He tells me that he loves me but isn't "in love" with me. I can't understand his response at all. Why would you stay with someone for more than a year if you weren't in love with them? I don't know what to do or where to go from here.

We struggle on for a couple more months, but it's tense and we're no longer happy and carefree like we used to be. Vincent finally tells me that he just doesn't think he's ever going to be able to give me what I want and ends our relationship. I am completely devastated. Our breakup is so much more painful than when either one of my marriages ended. I really loved him, and after he's gone, I pretty much just isolate myself. If I'm not working, then I'm at home alone.

\*\*\*

After a few months, I finally start getting out and enjoying myself a little bit again. Vincent hears that I've been seen out and about again, and he tries to get in touch with me. I refuse at first. I've been down the reconciliation road before, and it definitely didn't end well. Even though I miss him desperately, I can't imagine going through that hurt again.

After several more weeks, I finally agree to meet up with him, and he tells me that since we've been apart, he's realized that he does love me. He says that he has misses me so much and begs me to get back together with him. I tell him if we do then it's all or nothing. I want us to live together and commit to each other completely. He agrees, but he wants a bigger house, so I sell my tiny place and we buy a house together.

Aside from a few bumps in the road here and there, we are very happy together for more than three years. By this time it's 2014. I'm thirty, and Vincent is thirty-two. And he starts talking about wanting to have children. When our relationship became serious a few months after we first started dating, I told him about my inability to have children and said that if he had a desire to be a father, he shouldn't get more involved with me. He was adamant that he didn't want to have children and that being an uncle to his niece and nephew was all he would ever need. Now, out of nowhere, he decides he wants children of his own.

I tell him that he knows that's not possible for me, and he says he just wants to try. I made peace with the fact that I would never have children a long time ago, and I have no desire to "try" only to be disappointed again. He's not happy to hear this, and our relationship starts to suffer. He tells me that I'm being selfish and is angry with me a lot of the time. I'm really hurt and start to avoid being with him. Infertility is not a choice, and it's not something I would wish on anyone, so I'm angry too.

We start to fight a lot, and the relationship deteriorates quickly. We split up, and I'm devastated all over again. We sell the house, and I move into a smaller house close by. Vincent moves all the way across the country to California. I hear, through mutual friends, that he got married less than a year after we broke up and that they were trying to start a family right away. Guess he got what he wanted.

***

After Vincent and I split up, I stay single for a while. I can't even think about getting involved with anyone at this point. I feel like Vincent was truly the love of my life, and I can't seem to get over him. I date and have a few short-term relationships, but I never feel like I really "click" with anyone enough to pursue anything more. I focus more of my time on work and exercise. I also enroll in a cooking class and start taking Yoga. I'm keeping busy, but I feel like I need to make a big change in my life.

Liz and I had always talked about living in a warm climate, and we always complained about the frigid Midwest winters. In 2016 she and her family move to Nevada, just outside of Las Vegas. About a year later, I'm questioning why I'm still living in Iowa. It's freezing cold outside, and aside from some good friends, I can't come up with a single reason not to move where it's much warmer—and I'd be close to my best friend again. I start applying for jobs in Nevada, and the first offer I get is from Dr. Brandon Taylor. He owns a small but thriving dental practice about ten miles outside of Las Vegas. I accept the job, pack up, and move.

I'm having a great time living close to my best friend again, and I love my job. But being alone every night is difficult, and I long to have someone to share my life with. I date here and there and have one serious boyfriend, but that relationship ends very badly after about six months. I'm getting discouraged and think that I won't ever find someone to share my life with.

# CHAPTER 7
# 2019

Aside from a disastrous six-month relationship, I've been single for five years now. I'm thirty-five and trying online dating for the first time. I feel like it's really the only way to meet people at this point. Everyone has become so obsessed with their phones, and socializing seems to be a thing of the past.

I have a few lame dates and get ghosted multiple times. My subscription to the dating service is about to expire, and I decide that I'm not going to renew it. It's just not working for me at all, and I'm tired of talking to a bunch of strangers and having it go absolutely nowhere.

Right before the subscription expires, I get a typical "Hi, how are you?" message from someone. He's handsome, and I decide I'll give it one last shot and respond. We start talking. A lot. After talking to each other for hours over the next couple of weeks, we decide to meet up for a "proper" date. He wants to take me to dinner, but I suggest just meeting for a drink instead. I figure if you commit to just having a drink together and want to get away, it's much easier than suffering through dinner with someone if things aren't clicking.

I pick a small bar/restaurant, and I'm adamant about meeting in the early afternoon. I'm waiting in the parking lot and see him pull in. He's driving a nice car and looks even more handsome in person. He doesn't see me, so I let him walk in first and I walk in right after him. We see each other in person for the first time, and I *like* what I see.

We hug, and he tells me I look great. We sit down at a table and order a glass of wine. The conversation flows easily. Before I know it, we've each had two glasses of wine, appetizers, and dinner. What I thought would be an hour or less has turned into more than eight hours. I'm surprised they didn't ask us to leave! When we part company in the parking lot, he's a complete gentleman and only gives me a quick hug goodbye. I drive home feeling hopeful for the first time in what seems like forever.

We have a lot in common, and our relationship goes full steam ahead. My only hesitation is his job. He's does sales for a large medical device company, works long hours, and has to travel quite a bit. My hours are much more structured. The dentist's office is open from eight to five-thirty Monday through Thursday, and I never have to travel. I can even do my continuing education online. But I dismiss my concerns because I reason that I'd rather have someone who works hard than the opposite. So many of the guys I've gone out with barely work part time, and they complain about having to do that.

Even after all the shitty relationships I've had, I still believe in romance—the whole sending flowers, walks on the beach, and love notes kind of relationship. And at the beginning, Noah is very romantic. He sends me flowers often and takes me on little weekend getaways. I finally feel like I might be in a completely healthy relationship for the first time in my life.

Noah is four years older than me and was married once before. It lasted for twelve years, and he says it was never really a happy union because they just weren't compatible. He tells me that a truly happy marriage is what he has always wanted. And for me, the best part is that he has no desire to have children. He's thirty-nine and tells me that children are something he and his wife discussed early in their marriage, but they determined that it wasn't what either one of them wanted. He tells me he's very content with his child-free life. This is music to my ears.

After almost a year together, we start to talk about marriage. After my second divorce, I swore that I would never get married again. But after a year and a half, we are both confident that this is what we want for the rest of our lives. We get married at City Hall because neither one of us wants to have a wedding. Not to mention, it's late 2020 and the pandemic is still keeping people from being able to gather together anyway.

The marriage is good the first year or so, but it's also challenging because of the pandemic. It's made it very difficult to travel or just basically go out anywhere. I am dedicated to working out, but all the gyms are closed, so I find a series of old workout DVDs online and order them. I start working out at home and find that I actually enjoy it more than going to the gym. But aside from that, Noah and I are both dying to get out in the world and start doing things again.

We have no other choice but to spend our time working and just hanging out at home, and we're both bored and restless. As much as we love spending time together, it's just too much time together. Not to mention I'm sick of always having to be around Noah's dog, Max. He's an Italian Greyhound, and he's small and cute, but the breed is known for their need for constant attention and affection from their owners.

Now don't get me wrong, I'm a huge animal lover, but he's really over the top about the dog. He's constantly talking about him, playing with him, and taking pictures of him. Max has torn up some furniture in the house, and at night he is constantly in Noah's lap or laying between us while we watch television. It's really annoying to me.

Before we got married, we continued to live in separate houses. I decided early on that I wanted to do this relationship right, so we didn't sleep at each other's places. So I didn't know how attached he was to Max until after we got married.

It's pretty tough to cuddle with your husband when there's always a dog between you. Sometimes I put Max in another room and close the door, but then we have to listen to him whimper. Noah says that he feels guilty about putting him in the next room, so I have no choice but to share my husband with the dog every night. I could fight about it, but I don't want to feel like I have to beg Noah to give me attention. So I just read or zone out on TV while he sits with the dog.

I start to believe that I want too much and decide that I just need to suck it up and realize that this is what marriage is supposed to be like—full of compromises. I tell myself that I probably expect too much because of all my bad relationships in the past. After all, Noah is a kind and caring man, and he is devoted to me.

# CHAPTER 8
# 2023

It's three thirty on Sunday afternoon, and I'm waiting in the cell phone lot at the airport. Noah's plane has just landed, and I'll be picking him up in just a few minutes.

I feel so bad. I feel guilty and think that he will be able to see it written all over my face. I reason with myself that he couldn't possibly know I spent time with another man two days ago. But even though it was just a cup of coffee and conversation, I know I shouldn't have been there. I decide that I won't do it again and will go to that market any time but Friday afternoons from now on.

My text alert goes off—Noah is ready for me to pick him up. I pull up and greet him with a big hug. He says he missed me and gets in the car. He sits down and sighs loudly.

As I pull away from the curb, he says, "I'm so tired, and the flight was awful." I get to hear every detail about how the guy sitting next to him on the plane hogged the armrest and, again, how he didn't like the hotel he stayed in, and how he's so exhausted he thinks he'll be going to bed by eight o'clock.

I shouldn't be worried about him noticing any sort of guilty look on my face because he's yet to ask me how my day has been, or anything else for that matter. He literally complains until I pull into our driveway forty minutes later.

When he rambles on like this, I sometimes respond by saying something snarky like, "My day was fine, thanks for asking." And then he'll apologize for talking too much and ask me how my day was. But today I feel like I deserve to be ignored, so I just tell him that I'm sorry he had a bad trip and that I'm glad he's home.

When we get in the house, he immediately runs to Max. He picks him up and tells him how much he missed him and loves him. After ten minutes of throwing a tennis ball to the dog, he takes his laptop out of his bag and tells me he has to check his email. I start making dinner and pour us each a glass of wine.

We sit down to dinner, and for the third time now, he rehashes the details of the trip for me. I nod and occasionally interject with something like, "That must have been awful" or "Sorry you had to put up with that on the plane," but most of the time I just nod along while he's talking. But tonight as I'm nodding along, all the while I'm picturing a guy with beautiful blue eyes sitting across from me at a coffee shop, asking *me* questions and listening intently to my responses. Not fair to Noah, I silently scold myself. Jordan is a stranger, and when you first meet someone, you're always on your very best behavior, right?

I realize Noah is snapping his fingers in front of my face. "Hello, Earth to Kate." I snap out of my trance, apologize, and tell him that I was just thinking about how busy it's going to be at work tomorrow and that I have a particular client coming in that gets on my nerves because he's so picky.

He responds by saying, "Aww, look how cute he is!" He's looking at Max, who's curled up in his dog bed with his favorite toy tucked under his paw. I sigh, agree that he's adorable, and get up to put the dishes in the dishwasher. After the kitchen is cleaned up, I top off my glass of wine and sit down on the couch next to Noah. Max immediately leaves his dog bed and jumps in Noah's lap. Noah does make it past his predicted eight o'clock bedtime but not by much. He takes Max for a walk at about eight thirty and then goes to bed. I stay up and read for a while, but I can't really concentrate on my book at all. I keep wondering what Jordan is doing right now.

***

Monday, Tuesday, and Wednesday are pretty routine. Work, errands, cooking, and cleaning. Nothing out of the ordinary. Noah calls me on my lunch break on Wednesday to tell me that he has to go out of town for work again this coming weekend. He'll be leaving on Thursday evening and says he will just take an Uber to the airport so I won't have to drive home after dark and in rush hour traffic, which really is very sweet and considerate of him.

# CHAPTER 9
# 2023

It's Friday morning. Noah calls to say good morning. He lets me know that he'll be in meetings all day and that I probably won't hear from him again until bedtime. He'll call me then. I tell him to have a good day and that I'll talk to him later tonight.

    I pour myself a second cup of coffee, work out, and take a shower. I'm very well aware that it's Friday, but I keep telling myself that I'm *not* going to the market this afternoon. I put on my makeup and do my hair. I've started noticing a few gray hairs popping up over the past couple of years. My hair is naturally light brown, but I've been having my hairstylist add blonde highlights to it for as long as I can remember. The blonde really helps to hide the gray. I had it colored about four weeks ago, and, thankfully, I don't see any gray showing yet. After I blow-dry it I use my flat iron to add some loose waves. When I'm finished I take Max out for a quick walk. I'm going through the mail when I get back but can't concentrate on what I'm looking at. I finally admit to myself that I'm absolutely going to the market, and I think I've known it since I woke up this morning.

I'm trying to decide what to wear and realize that I haven't thought about what I'm wearing for a long time. Noah and I don't do much outside of the house, so I never give my clothes much thought anymore. If we're out and about, it's only to run errands. We've pretty much stopped doing much of anything else. If we do go out to eat, it's a last-minute decision, so I just go in my yoga pants and T-shirt.

He never plans any "dates" in advance anymore. Early in our relationship, Noah was always planning things for us to do—dinners, movies, day trips, hiking. He liked to surprise me, and I felt like he was really romantic. I know that it's not the man's responsibility to plan everything, and I used to do a fair amount of planning dates too. I guess I stopped doing it because after I saw no effort from him for months, I just sort of gave up. So here we are, in a complete rut.

When I did try to suggest going to an event or a movie, he was always too busy with work and would say something like, "Yeah, I'd like to see that movie, but I have to do some work this weekend," or he would have to travel and would tell me we'd go the following weekend, but it never happened. Then I'd remind him again a few weeks later, but by that time, the movie was no longer in the theater. I'm so frustrated with his lack of effort, so now I'm not trying either.

I go in my closet and pull out multiple options, trying on several different combinations of jeans, T-shirts, tank tops, and shorts. It's late July and over ninety degrees outside, but it's cold in the market, so jeans might not be a bad idea. I keep finding things I don't like about everything I put on. My thighs look too big in the shorts, my jeans make my butt look big, my arms look fat in the tank tops…and the list is endless. In my head I'm yelling, "Stop being so hard on yourself!" I know why I do it, but I also know that I shouldn't.

I settle on my favorite bootcut jeans and a fitted sleeveless top. I briefly consider leaving my ring at home, but I feel a wave a guilt wash over me and decide against that. I spend the next hour doing a little cleaning up in the house. I'm trying to distract myself with laundry and vacuuming. I keep thinking that maybe time will get away from me, the clock will pass two, and I won't go.

Not a chance. I'm looking at my watch every ten minutes.

# CHAPTER 10
# 2023

I let Max out one more time and fill his food and water bowls. I grab my purse and keys, and I'm walking out the door by 1:20. There's not much traffic, and I pull into the market parking lot at about 1:45.

When I pull in, I see what I think is Jordan's car, a dark blue Audi, at the back of the lot. My heart begins to race, and I immediately start to sweat a little bit. He must already be inside, I think, so I take a quick look in the mirror and put a mint in my mouth. I take a couple of deep breaths and put my hand on the door handle.

Wait. What am I going to "pretend" to shop for this week? I can't just buy the same five or six nonperishables I bought last Friday, can I? I scramble to make a quick mental list and decide that I'll get some coffee creamer, because we actually do need it and because maybe this will be just a completely run-of-the-mill trip for groceries, with no coffee break this time. Maybe Jordan won't even acknowledge me, maybe he has no intention of ever seeing me again, maybe he's had time to realize that last Friday probably should have never happened.

I'm going over so many scenarios in my head that a full five minutes goes by. I finally get out of my car, grab a basket, and go inside. I don't see him when I get into the store, but I convince myself I'm not looking. I pick up a loaf of bread and a box of crackers, and then I head to the dairy section to get the cream. And then I see him.

He's looking at a display of precut vegetables and fruit. He looks up, and then our eyes catch each other. I can tell immediately that he's happy to see me.

"Hi, Kate. It's good to see you," he says with a grin.

I smile back. "Hi, Jordan. It's good to see you too."

We stand there for a moment, and I don't think he's thought about what comes next any more than I have. I grab the coffee creamer and put it in my basket. We wordlessly begin to walk the aisles together, like we're here together. It feels really weird but really good too. I don't pick up any other groceries. I'm just enjoying walking next to him. That same old feeling of guilt washes over me, and I try to just push it aside. We make a little small talk about how our week was as we make our way to the checkout.

Once we are done, he asks me if I'd like to have coffee again. He says he has a cooler in the trunk of his car and I can put my creamer in there so that it won't get warm. I tell him that I'd like that and follow him to his car. I know what I'm doing is wrong, but at the same time I feel an intense rush of excitement. I put the creamer in the cooler, and we head over to the coffee shop.

I'm even more nervous this time than I was last Friday. It must be written all over my face because he says, "Everything okay, Kate? You look so serious."

I realized I've got my jaw clenched and my hands are balled into fists. I immediately relax a little and apologize. "Sorry, I guess I was just preoccupied for a minute."

We take a seat, and he gets us each a cup of coffee. There's a little more small talk before he suddenly says, "I have to say something. I don't know what you've been thinking or even if you've been thinking about last Friday but I've been thinking about you, Kate. And I know it's wrong because you are married, so I was really conflicted about what I would do if I saw you again or even if I should go to the market today.

"I don't know anything about your relationship or, frankly, you, for that matter. Maybe you do this often, maybe you're just unhappy in your marriage, or maybe this is the first time you've ever spent time with another man since you got married. Sorry, I know I'm rambling, but I'm really confused as to why either one of us is here. Like I said last Friday, I was married before, and I would have been devastated if I found out my wife was spending time with another man."

I don't say anything for a few seconds and try to take in what he just said. Finally I respond. "Well, Jordan, I've been thinking about you too. No, I've never done this before. I've always looked down on anyone who would do this to their spouse, so I do feel like a hypocrite sitting here with you. I just want to set the record straight and tell you that my husband is a good guy, actually a great guy, but for the past year, our marriage has been suffering. There is zero romance, and he's obsessed with work. I've tried all kinds of things to make it better—books, weekend getaways that he can never commit to because of work, marriage counseling, sexy lingerie—"

I realize I'm divulging *way* too much information, so I pause, clear my throat, and say, "I think you get my point. I certainly don't want to come off as some bored wife that was *looking* for another man to spend time with. But like you said last week, I don't know how to explain it. I just knew that I wanted to see more of you the instant I saw you in the store that first time."

He looks like he's suddenly relaxed and seems relieved by what I've just said. We drink our coffee, the mood lightens up significantly, and now we are just talking like two good friends. He asks me where Noah is now, and I tell him that he is out of town working. I think he can tell that I'm uncomfortable talking about Noah, so he quickly changes the subject. He's very interested in me and my work, and it is so refreshing to have someone actually focus all of their attention on me for a change. He asks me a ton of questions about where I'm from, my favorite food, favorite movie, etc. In turn I ask him the same questions, and I'm more than happy to find that when he relaxes, he's really funny. He doesn't make stupid jokes; it's more like sarcasm and plenty of self-deprecating humor, which is very much like my own. We spend about an hour talking, and then he asks me if I've tried the seafood place that's right across the street.

"No," I say, "but I've heard that it's really good."

I've asked Noah if we could go there several times since it opened, and he promises me that we will, but something, usually work, always seems to get in the way. He even goes as far as making a reservation for us one Friday night, but he didn't get home from work in time for us to make it. I was waiting, dressed up, sitting there watching the time go by, getting more and more angry by the minute. The reservation was for 6:00, and he comes in the door at 6:35. The worst part is that when he walks in, he just says, "Hey. What are you dressed up for?"

"Seafood restaurant. Does that ring a bell for you?" He apologizes multiple times, says it totally slipped his mind and he will definitely make it up to me. I silently go to the bedroom and change into sweatpants and an old T-shirt. When I come out, he's sitting on the floor playing with Max like nothing happened. That was over two months ago, and there's been no effort to "make it up" to me.

My thoughts are interrupted by Jordan saying, "Well, the crab cakes are supposed to be phenomenal, and I'm really hungry. Would you like to get something to eat with me, Kate?" I don't even hesitate and tell him that I would love to.

Since the restaurant is right across the street, we just walk over. As we are walking, I worry momentarily about the possibility of seeing someone I know, but I quickly dismiss that thought. It's not likely, and besides that, I don't owe anyone an explanation as to who I'm with. It's early, a little after four, so we get right in. They seat us in a small, two-seater booth, and I'm liking the ambiance—it's dimly lit with candles on the tables and pretty décor, not walls covered in fish nets and pictures of boats like most seafood places. The waitress brings us our menus and asks if we want anything from the bar. I ask for a Chardonnay, and Jordan tells her he'll have the same. She gives him a bigger smile than she gave me and says she'll be right back with our drinks.

They just opened for dinner at four, so it's happy hour right now. We each decide to get the shrimp cocktail appetizer off the happy hour menu to start with. The wine and shrimp cocktails arrive, and it's good, really good. We take our time with our appetizers, and then we both order the crab cakes.

I can't stop looking at him. He's beyond handsome, and those eyes! They are extra gorgeous in this candlelight. I try not to stare. But I can't help but wonder why someone so damn good looking is sitting here with me. Average-looking me.

"Kate, why are you shaking your head?"

I had no idea that I was actually shaking my head and say, "Oh, sorry, I was just thinking about something else. My mind was wandering for a second, but I'm back now." Inside I'm scolding myself—calm down!

I'm totally blown away when he says, "You are truly beautiful Kate. You're one of those women that every guy in the room can't help but look at when you walk in."

I can feel my cheeks turn red. "Oh come on, I really don't think that's true, Jordan." I'm even more flustered when he reaches across the small table and takes my hand.

"Look at me, Kate. I'm serious. You are beautiful. But it's more than that. You're warm and funny, and you just have that indescribable quality that people gravitate to and want to be around."

I can feel myself blushing, and I don't even know what to say to this so I whisper, "Thank you, Jordan. That might be the nicest thing anyone has ever said to me." I feel myself about to tear up, so I quickly try to lighten the mood "Have you looked in the mirror lately? I mean, you are like movie star good looking. And if you don't believe me, just check out how our waitress can't quit looking at you."

To my surprise his cheeks turn bright red too. "Wow, one glass of wine, and I think you must be drunk." We both laugh because neither one of us can seem to take a compliment very well. And it suddenly feels very comfortable between us.

Our crab cakes arrive and we eat and talk like we've known each other for years. Jordan asks if I'd like dessert, but I tell him no, thank you. It's after six now, and I really need to get going, so I tell him that we should head back to our cars. He insists on paying the bill, and we walk, very slowly, back to the parking lot.

I'm starting to feel sad that we have to say goodbye. Noah has worked two weekends in a row now, and I'm sure he'll be home next weekend. It might be weeks before see Jordan again. We're at his car now. He gets my coffee creamer out of his cooler, and I'm surprised to find that it's still ice cold.

"So, Kate," he says casually, "What are your plans for the weekend?" He's got his hands tucked in his pockets again, and he's swaying from side to side a little.

"I'm alone this weekend, so I really don't have anything planned. I'll spend some time on my patio reading, and since the weather is supposed to be beautiful tomorrow, I'll probably go for a long walk in the early afternoon."

"Do you ever go hiking?" he asks.

"I do, but not when I'm alone. Even though I always carry mace with me, I don't think it's a good idea for anyone, especially a woman, to hike all alone."

He nods. "Have you ever hiked any of the trails in Whitewater Park?"

"Oh yeah, that's only about ten miles from here, right? I went out there once with my best friend, and I remember it was really beautiful." I'm thinking that he's just making conversation and is going to tell me that he's going hiking tomorrow. Then he looks like he's trying to decide if he should say something or not.

After a few seconds, I start to say, "Today was really nice, thank you for—" but I don't get the rest of my sentence out because he's interrupting me.

"Kate, would you want to go on a hike with me tomorrow? There's a trail I really like at Whitewater. It's an easy hike, and there's hardly ever anyone else out there because most people go to Crater Park." He's right. Crater Park is nice, but it's always so packed with people. Lots of bikes and wannabe athletes constantly huffing behind you because you are in the way of their run up the mountain.

"I'd really like that," I say, and we decide to meet at a bagel shop that's just a couple miles from the park at ten the next morning. He says he'll see me in the morning, we say goodbye, and I drive home. The guilty feeling is less than it was last week, but it's still there. Even with that nagging at me, I can't help but smile and sing along with the radio all the way home.

When I get back, I take Max out for a quick walk and get my backpack and hiking shoes out for the next day. At about eight thirty, Noah calls, and as soon as I see his name come up on my phone, I feel sick to my stomach. That guilty feeling is much more prominent now.

I try to sound cheerful when I answer. He says he's at the hotel and just had dinner from room service. I ask about his flight and how the room is this time. He tells me that the flight was fine and the room is just okay. As usual, I get the ten-minute explanation of how his day went and what he has to do tomorrow.

He's in Sacramento, which is where his company's home base is. He gets sent out to visit various clinics and hospitals around the area and has to do a lot of follow up, so that's why he has to make the trip to Sacramento so often. When we first got married, we talked about the possibility of moving there so he wouldn't have to travel as much. But their second-biggest office is in Las Vegas, so he would have been traveling here sometimes too. We decided that staying in the Las Vegas area made more sense for us financially, and I didn't want to leave my job either—I'm happy there.

"Uh huh, uh huh," I'm saying while he talks, and then he asks me how Max is and what I did today. I tell him that Max is fine, and that I just did the usual stuff I always do on my Fridays off. I feel like a terrible person. I'm anxious to get off the phone because talking to Noah makes me feel awful about spending time with Jordan. And it should! I'm married, and I never dreamed I wouldn't honor that commitment in every way.

But I also never dreamed I'd be so lonely in my marriage.

Thankfully he tells me that he's tired and wants to get ready for bed. He's going to be driving to multiple locations tomorrow, and then he has to have a late dinner with his boss. He tells me he probably won't be able to call me until later in the evening, and I offer to just give him a call when I go to bed tomorrow night.

"Love you," we each say, and I assure him that I will give Max a kiss goodnight for him before we hang up. I breathe a sigh of relief to be off the phone, and I think to myself that if I had Jordan's phone number, I might text him and cancel our hike for tomorrow.

# CHAPTER 11
# 2023

I've been awake since five o'clock, so I decide to get up and do a quick workout before I shower and put on my makeup. It's supposed to be warm and sunny, so it will be a great day to be outside. I put on my SPF, then get dressed in shorts, a tank top, and a baseball cap. I've got a small backpack, and I put four bottles of water in it along with my ID, a credit card, my phone, a hairbrush, some cash, and my lip gloss.

 I head out the door at around 9:15 because it's going to be about a thirty-minute drive to the bagel shop, and I'd much rather be early than late. I pull in just before 9:50, and Jordan's not here yet. A couple minutes later, he pulls in next to me. I get out of my car and go to his window. This is awkward because we didn't talk about whether we were going to drive together or separate. I ask him what he would prefer, and he suggests that I just ride with him; otherwise we'll both have to pay admission to get in to the park, and isn't that sort of a waste of money? I agree, grab my backpack, and get in the passenger seat.

 I tell him what a nice car he has, and I'm more than happy to see that it's spotlessly clean inside. I'm wondering if he always keeps it this way or if he spent time cleaning it out last night. I tell myself that it doesn't matter—and why am I even thinking about that?! But actually, it does matter to me. I'm a very organized person, and I like to keep my house clean and everything orderly. I've taken a lot of grief for it from my exes, and I have been told that I'm "obsessed" and "over the top." I bought that shit for a while, but now I know that I was just with guys who weren't neat and clean and tried to make me believe it was some sort of character flaw that I have. Assholes.

We get to the park and set out on a trail that is approximately six miles if you go all the way around.

"We don't have to do the whole six miles," Jordan says. "I usually do, but sometimes I just do half."

"No, I'm fine with doing the whole six." I'm thinking the more distance we hike, the longer I'll get to spend time with him. He looks great today—cargo shorts, another T-shirt that fits his body perfectly, and a baseball cap. He looks even younger in that baseball cap, and he is, for lack of a better word, adorable. I'm not sure how I can feel so comfortable and so nervous at the same time.

Jordan interrupts my thoughts. "Please don't take this the wrong way, but I like the fact that you aren't tall."

"No offense taken," I smile. "I'm barely five three, so I usually wear shoes that have some height to them. No hiding my height when I'm wearing tennis shoes."

I've put up with all kinds of rude comments about my height my entire life. A lot of times, people don't take me seriously, like I'm still a little kid. My favorite is when people laugh and say something like, "Oh my gosh, you're really short!" I think it's odd that it's somehow acceptable to make fun of someone's height, like anyone has a choice in the matter. His comment about my height doesn't sound like an insult at all though.

He goes on to say, "Most people think that all guys are like six two, and you wouldn't believe the rude comments that I've gotten because I'm five ten. I've had women actually tell me that they can't date me because they have a 'rule' that they won't date a guy shorter than six feet tall, and some of the women who said this to me were barely over five feet."

I can't believe that any woman wouldn't date this guy just because he doesn't meet a height requirement for them. I guess I had never thought about guys having to put up with that sort of crap too. And I honestly hadn't paid any attention to his height before now.

We're about a half a mile into the hike when we stop to have some water. It's a picture-perfect day—blue sky, sunshine, and a nice breeze, and I'm really enjoying myself.

I'm surprised when Jordan says, "You've got great legs, Kate. I can absolutely tell that you work out." He blushes and looks like he's sorry he just said that out loud.

I immediately say, "Nah, my legs are my least favorite thing about my body, but thanks." He looks a like he's a little hurt that I responded that way.

"You really don't know how beautiful you are, do you? I'm not sure why you don't see it in yourself, but believe me, you are exceptional."

Exceptional?! When has anyone ever told me that I'm *exceptional*? Um, never! "Careful, Jordan, you keep saying all these sweet things to me, and I might just have to keep you." I can feel my heart start racing about a million miles an hour. That had to be the stupidest sentence that has ever come out of my mouth, and I feel like I just want to disappear right now! He doesn't seem to notice at all and doesn't skip a beat when he responds.

"I might just be okay with that, Kate," he says, and then he gives me that big smile that makes my pulse race even more.

We continue to hike the full six miles, and it takes over three hours because we stop a lot along the way. We've finished all our water, and I really need to use the bathroom. Thankfully there are facilities at the park entrance, so we make our way back there and go inside. After I use the restroom, I take my hair out of the ponytail and brush it. Then I put on some lip gloss, reapply my deodorant (I always keep a travel size in my backpack), and head out. Jordan is leaning up against the wall waiting for me, and he's shaking his head with that same big smile on his face.

"What?" I ask.

"Well, you might be sick of hearing things like this from me, but how can anyone look that damn good after hiking six miles?"

I smile shyly and thank him. And I'm thinking, he can't possibly know how much I needed to hear that—and that I don't think I'll ever get sick of hearing him say things like that.

We get in his car and put the windows down. He turns on the radio, and he's got it set to a station that plays all '70s and '80s music, which is my favorite. Did he remember me telling him that at dinner last night, or is this just the station that he likes to listen to? Before I can ask, he says, "Does it bother you if I have the radio on? I'll keep the volume down, but I have to have good music on while I'm driving."

I tell him I don't mind at all and that I like his choice of music. It's only a little after two, and I'm happy knowing that we don't have to hurry home, unless he says he wants to. He asks me if I'd like to go to this little place called Boards and Bottles for a late lunch.

"No," I say, and he looks surprised. I smile and follow up with, "Unless you let me pay this time."

He starts to protest but then says, "If it's the only way you'll go to lunch with me, then I'll agree to your terms. Even though I'm not entirely happy about it." He gives me that big smile again, and I feel absolutely giddy.

We park, go inside, and ask for a seat on the patio. I order a Pinot Noir, he orders a Cabernet, and we decide to share a charcuterie board that has prosciutto, six types of cheese, fruit, and three types of bread. I tell Jordan that I think I could live on bread, cheese, and wine, and he says he agrees but would occasionally have to have a steak too.

I smile and say, "Okay, that's it, have you been having me followed or something? I absolutely love a good steak! A filet mignon with a glass of red wine is my favorite way to indulge."

"Well, I think this is where we disagree Kate. I'd have to say a really great ribeye with a glass of red wine is the very best way to indulge." There's that gorgeous smile again, and I tell him I think that won't be a deal breaker for our friendship. He agrees, and we smile at each other. I think we both know that we are already more than friends.

The wine and food arrive, and I realize how hungry I am. I had some toast at about six thirty this morning but nothing since then. We are both really enjoying the food, and we start talking about our diets and what we like to eat. He tells me that he believes in everything in moderation and eats when he's hungry but tries to keep it mostly healthy.

"I'm pretty strict most of the time," I tell him, "But I do indulge occasionally, especially after I've just hiked six miles. That deserves a piece or two of sourdough and some cheese!" I'm not sure why, but I blurt out that I used to be very overweight and that's why I'm so disciplined about my eating and workout habits.

"Really? I can't even imagine that when I look at you. You're very thin, Kate. I mean, you look great, and if anything, I'd say you could afford to weigh a little more."

"I appreciate you saying that because sometimes I still see that thirteen-year-old girl, sixty pounds overweight, staring back at me in the mirror."

He touches the top of my hand and says, "I'm so sorry that you ever had a time when you looked in the mirror and didn't see how spectacular you are."

I can feel a lump starting in my throat, but the last thing I want to do is cry.

# CHAPTER 12
# 1996

It's August in Iowa. It's hot and humid. I'm twelve years old, and I'm with my dad and his girlfriend. I'm looking at jeans, sweaters, and coats—hard to think about when it's ninety degrees and so humid outside that it makes you feel like you're wrapped in a hot, wet blanket.

But school starts in a couple of weeks, and part of my dad's child support obligation includes buying me back-to-school clothes every year. I will be wearing the sweaters in about two months and the coat in about three months, so what we're shopping for makes sense, but I'm hot and sweaty trying on all this stuff.

Gail, Dad's girlfriend, insists on me coming out and modeling every outfit I try on. I pull on a pair of size nine/ten jeans, and they're way too tight, but I'm determined to make them fit. So I suck in as much as I can and struggle to get the zipper up. I pull on a long-sleeved shirt and leave it untucked so they won't see that the jeans aren't buttoned and the zipper is only about a third of the way zipped. Then I put a heavy jacket over everything.

Gail is calling for me to come out of the dressing room, so I step out onto the platform that's surrounded by mirrors. "Take off the coat, Kate, so we can see the outfit!" she demands.

"I think everything fits fine," I say.

"Well, we're not going to buy the clothes unless we see them!"

First of all, I think, *you* aren't buying them, and second of all, why are you even here?! Reluctantly I unzip the coat and take it off, and I know what's coming.

Gail looks disgusted as she looks me up and down. She turns to my dad. "Paul, you absolutely can't buy those clothes for her. Look how fat she is!"

Tears well up in my eyes, and I just stand there, on display, because I don't know what else to do. I'm hoping my dad will tell her to be quiet, but that doesn't happen. Dad just nods in agreement and tells me to go back to the rack, find the same jeans two sizes larger, and try those on.

I hate Gail. She is a nasty bitch and treats me and my dad like shit. And Dad is a spineless wimp around her. He met her shortly after he and my mom divorced in 1992 and thinks she's somehow elegant and worldly because she lived in Italy for a couple of years, and he's never lived anywhere but the same small town in Iowa his whole life. I think she's just a phony witch. She doesn't even have a real job—she claims she's a "poet" and sits around writing shitty poems all day and judging other people who actually have to go to work for a living. Her husband passed away a few years ago and left her very well off, so she doesn't have to work.

Instead of being grateful for her comfortable lifestyle, she looks down on my dad because she thinks his job as an electrician isn't "fancy" enough for her. I never understood why my dad started dating her in the first place, and I think she continues to have a relationship with him just because she knows she can push him around.

I'm in the dressing room. Sobbing. I put the jeans on, and they fit fine, maybe even slightly roomy, but they are a size thirteen/fourteen. I've put on a lot of weight over the past couple of years. Puberty and the fact that I'm barely over five feet tall don't help. I was a painfully skinny kid, and Mom and Dad were constantly pushing food on me to try and get me to gain weight. I guess all the burgers, potato chips, and candy bars finally caught up to me, and now I'm about sixty pounds overweight.

My mom is certainly not mother of the year, but there is one thing I'll always give her credit for, and that's her never insulting me or making my weight an issue. If I was crying because I was being teased and bullied at school because of my weight, she would just say, "If there's something you don't like about yourself, then change it." She continued to let me eat as much as I wanted and never tried to force a diet on me. I guess she figured I'd handle it in my own way in time. And I did.

I come out of the dressing room with red eyes, wiping my nose. Gail rolls her eyes. "Stop crying. If you really cared about how you look, you'd go on a diet."

I silently wish her dead—I think the rest of the people standing within earshot do too—and look at my dad. He just says, "Those jeans look so much better. Go change and we'll pay for this stuff. And Gail's right, you really can't afford to get any bigger or pretty soon we'll have to buy your clothes at a 'big woman's' store."

You just had to get that last dig in there, didn't you, Dad? I was already as humiliated as I thought I could be but he just had to take it to one more level. When we leave the store, Dad slips me a twenty-dollar bill, which is always his way of apologizing, and offers to take me to dinner. Dinner? Are you kidding?! I tell him I'm tired and don't feel like going to dinner, and he and the witch are more than happy to drop me off at home. When I get home, I grab a bag of potato chips and a soda and spend the rest of night in my room, crying and wishing I'd never been born.

My dad has never really been what I'd call a dad. I think he tries sometimes, but he is just not the nurturing type at all and his temper is off the charts—just ask my mom. I've been on the receiving end of his temper many times. He's especially hard on me because of my weight and has no trouble telling me I'm fat and I'll never have a boyfriend as long as I'm overweight. He's gotten worse with the insults since he started dating the witch. She didn't like me from day one and views me as an inconvenient embarrassment that she occasionally has to put up with. Did I mention that I despise her? Witch!

My dad does feel remorse, but it's only after he's screamed at me, insulted me, and made me cry. I can't even count the times that he's berated me on the phone until I cry and hang up on him only to have him call right back five minutes later, apologizing profusely and offering to buy me something. I'd much rather have a dad than the stuff, but I take the guilt gifts, like money and later a car, because I know he is never going to be a father to me.

# CHAPTER 13
# 2023

I think Jordan's praise of me and how I look just brought up some old insecurities, I realize as I try to outrun the tears forming behind my eyes. I hadn't thought about my dad and the witch embarrassing me in public for a really long time. I've learned, through a lot of therapy, how not to dwell on the past like I used to.

It's too soon to share all that with Jordan. Not only do I not want to share my traumatic memories with someone I barely know, but I also don't want to kill the mood. We're having a great day, and the last thing I want to do is spoil it by reliving a horrific memory from my fucked-up childhood.

I push that awful memory aside and try to concentrate on the fact that Jordan still has his hand resting on top of mine. I get control of myself, and thankfully I don't cry. I keep thinking he's going to move his hand away because it was just his way of consoling me when I looked like I was going to have a meltdown, but he seems to like how it feels, and I definitely do too.

We spend the next three-plus hours enjoying the warm afternoon together, and after we eat and finish our wine, we share a scoop of lemon gelato. We reluctantly make our way back to the lot where my car is parked. It's almost six, and I know I should be getting home. Max needs to be walked, and I have some things I need to do at home before bedtime.

We get back to the bagel shop, and I don't know what to say. I know that Noah will be home next weekend for sure, and I'm feeling sad that I can't do this again anytime soon. I tell him thanks again for a great day, and he thanks me for lunch.

We are both looking at the ground, and there is at least a full twenty seconds of silence, but then he says, "This is an unfair question, but when can I see you again, Kate? I shouldn't even be asking you that, and I'm mad at myself for it. But I would be lying if I said that I wasn't enjoying your company tremendously."

I sigh, and it's a sigh of relief. "It's okay to ask me that because I'm enjoying your company tremendously as well. I can't promise when I can see you again, but could I have your number? We can at least text each other during the day sometimes? Would that be all right with you?"

"Sure, but aren't you concerned that Noah might see your messages?"

I cringe a little at that question, but I know there is nothing to worry about. "Noah has never once looked at my phone or asked me who is texting or calling me. He is so caught up in work and the dog that I think I could be talking to you right in front of him and he wouldn't even notice."

Jordan looks reassured. I put his number in my phone and get out of the car. He gets out too and walks me to my car door. We again tell each other what a great day it's been, and I'm totally taken by surprise when he pulls me in for a hug.

"Hope to see you soon, Kate," he whispers in my ear as he holds me. "Drive carefully."

I can barely speak but manage to say, "You too."

He waits in his car until I give him a last quick wave and start driving away before he pulls out of the parking lot.

You ever drive somewhere and swear that you don't remember the drive at all? That's how I feel when I pull into my garage at home. I was thinking about that hug and the day with Jordan all the way home. As soon as I turn the car off, I am suddenly flooded with emotion, and I begin to cry. Hard. I am overwhelmed with so many different feelings; joy, guilt, fear, loneliness, and most of all, intense attraction for Jordan. I tell myself that I'm a terrible person, but I feel more alive than I've felt in over a year!

I pull myself together and go in the house. Max is whining in his kennel and needs to be walked. I left him food and water and put his pee pad down for him, but it's dry. He must really need to go. I immediately put the leash on him and take him for a walk around the block. He's grateful to be out, and I don't blame him. I take him off the leash and let him run in the grassy area for a while. I owe him that. When we get back to the house, I throw the tennis ball a few times for him, give him a couple of treats, and then he lays down in his favorite doggy bed.

It's 7:45, and I'm tired. I unload the dishwasher and go through the mail that's been on the counter since yesterday. Then I wash off my makeup, put on my pajamas, and curl up on the couch. I turn on the TV and start flipping through the channels, but I can't pay attention to anything that's on. I finally just turn the volume way down and try to read, but it's tough to pay attention to what I'm reading too.

I'd love to call Liz and talk this out with her. I want to tell someone how wonderful Jordan is and what a fantastic weekend I had, but I can't. I can't talk to anyone about this because I know that it's wrong. What would I expect her to say? That it's okay to spend time with another man while my husband is out of town?! No way! And I certainly wouldn't tell her it was okay for her if the situation were reversed. So I'm just going to have to deal with this on my own. And that makes it even harder.

My head hurts from thinking about all of it, and I decide it's time to go to bed. After I get in bed, I shut the light off and turn the television on, which is typically how I like to fall asleep when I'm home alone. I told Noah I would call him when I got in bed, so I do just that. He doesn't answer and it goes to voicemail. It's 9:45. He couldn't possibly still be out to dinner with his boss, could he? I don't leave a message and try to concentrate on television.

Less than ten minutes later, my phone rings and it's Noah. He apologizes and tells me that he was down the hall getting some ice when I tried to call. What does he need ice for at ten o'clock at night? We make small talk, and he tells me about dinner with his boss. He says that the boss is really pleased with how he's handling all his accounts and wants to give him even more responsibility. He says he'll tell me more about it when he gets home but he'll say goodnight for now. I'm glad because I'm about to fall asleep. We say our usual "love you." I hang up the phone and fall asleep almost immediately.

***

The next day is a typical Sunday. I pick up some groceries at the big market that's only a few blocks from my house and go to a couple of other stores. On Sunday Noah and I usually go to the wine market in town and pick up a couple of nice bottles for the week. I decide to go ahead and do that, and I spend quite a bit of time in there today looking at all the different choices. I finally settle on a Chardonnay and a Cabernet, and my mind immediately goes to my time with Jordan over the past two days. I really need to stop thinking about him. I have to go to the airport and pick up Noah at around four today, and I should only be concentrating on that.

When I get home, I wash and dry my uniforms for the workweek and then head out to pick up Noah. I literally cannot stop thinking about the past two days all the way to the airport, and that guilty feeling is in full force when I pull in to the passenger pick-up area.

I get out of the car, and Noah is practically running to me. What? This isn't like him. Not that he wouldn't hug me, but he looks almost—what's the word I'm looking for? Elated.

He gives me a big hug and says, "I really missed you, Kate!"

Usually his first words are "How's my Max?" but not today. I tell him I missed him too, and then he gives me a kiss. I'm thinking, who are you and what did you do with Noah?

Someone is honking for us to move, so I say, "We'd better get going," and we get back in the car. As we are driving away from the airport, he puts his hand on my shoulder and says, "It's so good to be home." And I feel like the worst person on Earth!

When we get home, I tell Noah that I've got some grilled chicken in the fridge and a salad that I made earlier for dinner tonight. He's playing with Max and tells me that sounds good and he's hungry. I pour us each a glass of Chardonnay, and we sit down at the dining room table.

"Well...," I start, "what's the news about your job?" I asked him on the ride home from the airport, but he said he wanted to wait and talk about it when we got home. All I can think is that I hope he isn't going to tell me that his company wants us to relocate. I can't even think about that now.

"Well, there's good news and bad news." Of course there is. "The bad news is that after next weekend, I'm going to have to travel for at least the next six to eight weekends." I feel really bad because my first thought is that I don't like that at all. I already hate how much he travels. But my next thought is that I'm ecstatic about the possibility of getting to spend more time with Jordan. I'm the worst.

"The good news is that I got a promotion, a 10 percent raise, and a bonus!"

"Wow, honey, that's great! I'm so happy for you!" And that really is true. He works hard, and I know he's been wanting to move up in the company. He spends the next half hour telling me about the dinner with his boss and how he was offered the promotion. The company is taking on some new territory, opening new offices, and he needs to go and establish his accounts in person. He'll be traveling to Texas, Florida, Tennessee, and South Carolina over those six to eight weekends.

He finally says, "I know it will be tough for a few weeks, but this is going to be great for me financially." *For me*, I think, not for *us*? But I dismiss the thought because I know that's just how he always thinks. He was single for a long time before me and has a hard time thinking in the plural sometimes.

I decide I'm not going to dwell on having to do everything at home by myself every weekend for the next two months, including walking Max at least twice a day, and tell him I'm very proud of him and that we'll make it work.

We spend the next hour sitting at the table with him talking about work and showing me on his computer where the new offices are located. Max needs to be walked before bedtime, and we both take him out. I tidy up the kitchen while he goes through his email, and we head off to bed a little early. We both read for a short time, he gives me a quick kiss goodnight, and then he rolls over to go to sleep.

We haven't been intimate in over six months, so this is nothing new. But I can't help but feel like we are drifting further and further apart. I don't know what changed, or maybe this is just a normal "dry spell" that a lot of couples go through? I don't really have any healthy relationships for reference, so I just decide to be patient and wait for things to return to normal. I tried talking to him about it about a month ago, and he assured me that things are just "crazy busy" right now; he's exhausted, and it has nothing to do with me. He told me that I don't need to read self-help books, we don't need to go to counseling, and I need to stop worrying. After that, I decided not to push the issue.

# CHAPTER 14
# 2023

The alarm is going off. It's five o'clock, and it's a workout morning for me. Some mornings I'd much rather sleep an extra forty-five minutes, but I'm committed to my routine. After I finish my workout, I shower, put on my makeup, and dry my hair, and now I'm sitting at the table having my usual breakfast. Noah comes out of the bedroom and takes Max out for his morning walk. When he gets back, he showers and has breakfast, and then we both head out for work.

When I get to the office, I get all my supplies ready and set up my tray for my first patient of the day. I go up to the front desk to see if my 8:15 appointment has arrived yet. She hasn't, but there is one woman sitting in the waiting area. She's got her head down, but I can see that her jaw looks swollen. They tell me that my 8:15 just canceled because of car trouble and ask me if I can please take the woman in the waiting room back for X-rays. She looks nervous and upset, and I think they want to get her out of the waiting room as soon as possible so she feels more comfortable. I tell them I'd be happy to.

I look at the name at the top of her registration form and quietly say, "Amy, would you like to come with me? I'm Kate, and I'll be taking your X-rays before you see Dr. Taylor."

She stands up and follows me to the back of the office. I look at her chart and see that she's here for a consult to fix two broken teeth. I ask her about any possibility of pregnancy, go over her medications and medical history—all the usual questions we ask before we use radiation. I tell her that I will let her know how to turn her head for each image, put the lead apron on her, and go behind the curtain. I tell her to turn left, then right, and then raise her chin a little. When she does that I can see bruises all along her jaw and small bruises on her neck.

After the X-rays are complete, I take her to the exam room and bring the images up on the screen. Both of her front teeth are broken, and two of her molars are cracked. She asks if I see anything more than the two broken teeth that she's already aware of, and I tell her that Dr. Taylor will go over her X-rays with her.

Tears are suddenly rolling down her cheeks. I hand her a box of tissues and ask her if she's all right. Her hands are shaking as she takes the tissues. She doesn't look at me and says she's fine, but she's obviously not fine at all. I pull up the stool next to her and ask if there's anything else I can get her. She says no and apologizes for crying.

"Please, don't apologize. It's really okay. I just wish I could help."

"I'm sure you've figured out what happened to me," she says.

I just nod. I don't want to make her feel worse by saying it out loud, but I knew what happened to her the minute I saw the bruises and the look of embarrassed defeat on her face. And now I'm trying not to cry right along with her.

She takes a deep breath. "I'm not one of these women, you know? I don't allow guys to beat on me. With him it just started gradually after we'd already been together for almost a year, like insults here and there, and he slapped me in the face once. But after he did it, he cried, apologized like a million times, and said he's not 'that guy' and he didn't know what came over him. He said he was just stressed and promised it would never happen again. I had moved in with him just two months before and had sold almost all my stuff when I did."

I nod again and tell her I understand. I want to tell her that I had someone give me that same speech, almost word for word, but I grit my teeth and stay quiet.

She goes on to say, "And it didn't happen again for almost three months. But two days ago, he came home from work and saw me talking to our neighbor. I was out getting the mail, and the neighbor guy came out to get his mail, and we started talking. He was asking me if I'd heard that the HOA fee in our neighborhood was going up, and we were just talking about that when Rick, my boyfriend, got home from work. He pulled the car into the garage and came over to the mailbox. It didn't look like anything was bothering him at all. He was smiling and put his arm around me. He stood and talked to the neighbor about the HOA and a couple of other things going on in our subdivision. Then we went inside." She takes a deep breath to catch her voice before continuing.

"I said that I was going to start dinner and asked him if he would mind lighting the grill. I was completely blindsided when he said to me, "You think I don't know that you're fucking Nathan?!" I couldn't believe that he'd just accused me of having a relationship with our *married* neighbor, and I didn't know what to say." She shakes her head at the memory, eyes aimed at the ground.

"He was coming at me with his fist raised, and all I could think to do was scream, 'No, please, I swear I didn't do anything.' But he didn't even pause. He just started punching me, and I know he hit me at least five or six times before I dropped to the ground and curled up in a ball. I was hysterical, you know? Crying and begging him to stop. And the next thing I know, *he's* crying, telling me how sorry he is and trying to help me up." My own eyes start to swell with tears as I think about what this woman's been through.

"I know I should have gone to the police, but I just couldn't do it. I went to the ER and gave them a story about how I fell down a short flight of concrete stairs and smacked my jaw on the bottom step. They asked if anyone else was there when it happened, and I lied and told them, 'No, I live by myself,' and they seemed satisfied with that. They took X-rays and referred me here." By this time she's crying pretty hard, and I try to comfort her by telling her that, in the past, I was in the exact same type of situation as her.

"Please listen to me, Amy. I know how hard it is to leave, but you need to get out *now*. I want you to come back and meet me in the parking lot during my lunch hour so I can give you some information. Let me help you." Before she can respond, Dr. Taylor is standing in the doorway, and he doesn't look happy.

"All finished up here, Kate? I need to go over the X-rays with the patient."

"Yes, all done," I say while standing. I leave the exam room.

Right before I take my 9:15 patient back, Dr. Taylor pulls me aside.

"I heard you talking to her, Kate. You can't cross a line like that. I'm required to report this because I suspect domestic violence, but you can't get involved in it personally." He's right. Dr. Taylor is a great boss, and he is a kind and generous guy, so if he's giving me a little slap on the hand, then I know I've got it coming.

"You are absolutely right, and I apologize. I feel really bad for her, and I guess I was just trying to help. It won't happen again, Dr. Taylor."

He looks concerned but gives me a smile, and it reassures me that he's not mad at me. "You don't know how much it sickens me when I hear stories like hers and see those bruises on her face, but we have to follow the rules. I appreciate how much you care about people, Kate, I really do. Now, you're 9:15 is waiting." He gives me a wink and a big smile and goes back to his office.

From twelve until almost one, I sit and eat lunch in my car, but as much as I hoped she would, Amy doesn't come back.

# CHAPTER 15
# 1989

I'm five years old. My home life has become complete chaos, and my parents are constantly fighting. My mom, who used to be such a great mother, has completely changed. She's acting like she's twenty-one years old again—running around and leaving my sister and me alone at night, and at thirty-eight, she has suddenly taken up smoking and drinking. That perfect mom that we had is quickly disappearing before our eyes, and I am so confused.

My sister Jessica, who is thirteen years older than me, just moved out, so it's just me and my sister Morgan, who is five years older than me, at home now. My parents have been married for nineteen years and unhappy for at least the past ten.

My dad is eleven years older than my mom, smokes two packs of cigarettes a day, and is in a bad mood most of the time. He's an electrician by trade but has recently become a lineman and works out of town a lot. When he is home, he'd be more than happy to watch television and smoke every minute that he's awake. He has always had a temper, but it's become much worse over the past three or four years. I was not planned, and I'm pretty sure the divorce would have happened a lot sooner if I hadn't been born. On top of being an "accident"—that's what my older sister used to tell me to make me cry—I'm born with a lot of medical problems, which require multiple surgeries and extended stays in the hospital.

It's Thanksgiving. I've been very sick, which is just the norm at this point, and have been sleeping in my room off and on all day. I hear yelling and slowly make my way down the hall. I walk around the corner just in time to hear my dad tell my mom she's a "fucking slut." He picks up the glass that he's been drinking whiskey out of and throws it at Mom. She sees what he's about to do and jumps up out of her chair right before the glass makes contact. It ends up hitting her right on the top of her hand. The glass breaks, and her hand is cut open and bleeding.

I am frozen in the doorway, and Morgan is sitting on the floor next to our mom and crying hysterically. Mom just gets a Band-Aid and puts it on the cut, which probably needed stitches, and goes in the kitchen to finish making Thanksgiving dinner.

Dad is immediately standing behind her, apologizing and asking what he can do to help with dinner. Mom is quietly crying, and Dad grabs some tissues and wipes the tears off her face. I hear him tell her that he wants to go shopping for a new car the next day, and he really wants her to pick it out—"You can get whatever you want. I know you've always wanted a red sports car, so that's what we're going to get. How's that? Does that make you happy?"

Mom manages a weak smile and tells him it does. She gets her red car, and Dad is trying to be overly nice. But the peace does not last long. Less than a month later, Dad is mad because some guy was talking to mom in the grocery store checkout lane. When we get home, he accuses her of flirting with the guy, and it ends with mom getting slapped across the face. These violent episodes always end the same. Mom cries, and Dad apologizes and offers to buy her something or take her on a trip. The slap gets us all a trip to the amusement park the following weekend. And the time he gave her a black eye—

well that one earned us a long weekend at the beach in South Carolina.

This pattern goes on for the next three years until they get divorced. In the meantime, Dad is having an affair with the married neighbor lady across the street, and Mom is having an affair with the much younger bartender at the club that she has been frequenting for the past couple of years.

***

It's 1991 and it's my seventh birthday. I'm in the hospital again, which isn't unusual. I've spent more than half my life in the hospital because I was born with some sort of defect in my bladder and kidneys. I keep getting small tears in the lining of my bladder, which have to be repaired. I also have a defect in one of my kidneys that causes a blockage, and I get frequent, painful bladder infections. When this happens I have to be admitted to the hospital for IV antibiotics and monitoring. When I'm not in the hospital, I'm on a maintenance antibiotic to try to prevent infections.

The doctors say that as I get older, when my growth spurts slow down, the tears in my bladder will happen a lot less often, and the condition should eventually resolve completely. I've had three surgeries on my right kidney and four surgical repairs done on my bladder. They even talked about removing my kidney about six months ago, but luckily the third surgery was successful, and they don't think I'll have to have any more surgery on it.

But the bladder is still a problem, and I'm here in the hospital on my birthday because two days ago, I developed another bladder infection and had a fever of 102 degrees. I'm crying because I've been alone all day, and I keep asking the nurses when my mom is going to come. Dad's working out of town, but Mom promised me the night before that she would come to the hospital the next day and she would bring me a chocolate cake for my birthday.

I can't guarantee it, but I'm pretty sure my favorite nurse, Wanda, called Mom and told her she needs to get here because her daughter is crying. The nurses' station is right across from my room, and I can hear Wanda raise her voice and say, "Well, visiting hours are over in less than two hours, so you need to get up here." She hangs up the phone and says to one of the other nurses, "I feel so sorry for Kate. Her parents have become so neglectful over the past couple of years."

Wanda is always so sweet to me whenever I'm having one of my hospital stays. I have to get stuck, a lot, and always request that she give me my shots and start my IVs. She is so gentle and always succeeds on the first stick. She was working last Christmas when I was admitted for a three-day stay, and she spent half of her shift playing games with me in my room, brought me candy canes, and watched television with me until I fell asleep. Mom had come to visit me and bring me my Christmas presents earlier in the day but said she could only stay for a little while because she had to get home to be with Morgan.

Mom finally comes to see me, about thirty minutes after I heard Wanda on the phone with her. But she's not alone. She has her recently divorced, party-girl friend, Jane, with her. I don't like Jane. She's obnoxious and does not like kids. She's only interested in going out, getting drunk, and picking up guys. Why is she here?! Mom and Jane are dressed up to go out, and that's obviously where they're headed after Mom pays me the required visit.

Mom hugs me and says, "Happy Birthday, Kate. I'm so sorry you have to spend it here in the hospital. But we'll celebrate better when you get home in a couple of days." I open my gifts—a Barbie and a Barbie car. I tell mom thanks, hug her, and say that I love my presents. Then I ask her if she brought my chocolate cake.

"I did bring you a cake, but it's not chocolate. Sorry, honey, all the bakery had left was pineapple upside down." I make a "yuck" face and ask Mom why she didn't bake my cake, like she's always done in the past.

Jane pipes up and says, "You know, your mom has a life too. She doesn't always have time to do things like that. Why don't you try saying thank you?"

Mom quietly says "Jane." She knows Jane is completely out of line but doesn't say any more. So I do.

I burst into tears and say, "Get out of here, Jane! I hate you, and I don't want you here!"

Jane just smirks, having gotten the reaction she wanted. "Okay, let's go, Lana," she says to my mom. I'm crying hysterically and begging Mom to stay and play with my new Barbie with me. Mom says that she'd love to stay, but visiting hours are going to end soon and Jane drove her, so she has to go. I'm still crying and begging her to stay when she hugs me and tells me she'll be back to see me first thing in the morning. With that, she and Jane leave. Obviously, the bar is much more important than your sick kid.

Right after they're gone, Wanda comes in with a piece of chocolate cake that has a single lit candle in it. She's followed by the other four nurses working on the floor, and they all sing Happy Birthday to me. I blow out the candle and eat my piece of cake.

"Show me what your mom bought you, Kate," Wanda says. I show her my new Barbie and car. She tells me that she has to go check on a couple other kids, but she'll be back in about twenty minutes and we'll play. In exactly twenty minutes she returns, and we play with Barbie, read, and color for about an hour. Wanda always keeps her promises. I feel a lot better. She wishes me a happy birthday again, tucks me in, and turns my overhead light off. Thank goodness there are people like her in this world.

***

It's about three months later when my parents start to really talk about splitting up, but I'm eight years old when they finally get a divorce. I'm home from school, as usual, because I'm not feeling well. It's early in the afternoon, and I'm sleeping in the bedroom at the back of the house.

I'm slowly waking up because someone is yelling. The yelling is getting louder and louder. I hear Dad yell, "Lying bitch!" Then there's a loud thud, and Mom is screaming. But she's not screaming in anger. It sounds like she's screaming in fear.

I get out of my bed and walk slowly to the kitchen. Mom is on the floor, and all I see is blood. Blood on the floor, blood on her shirt, blood on her pants, and blood pouring down the side of her head. There's so much blood.

Dad is bent down, pressing a towel to the side of Mom's head. He's saying, "Now you know I didn't hurt you. I just pushed you a little and you fell." Mom is nodding in agreement. Dad says he's going to get her some ice, and Mom is suddenly scrambling off the floor, picking up the phone and dialing 911. She manages to get our address out before Dad grabs the phone out of her hand and slams it against the wall, shattering the handset.

I start to cry and they both suddenly notice that I'm standing in the doorway of the kitchen. Dad says, "Everything's ok here, Kate. Go back to bed." No chance. I'm frozen in my spot.

I hear sirens, and within minutes the police are banging on the front door. Dad just calmly sits in his recliner as Mom lets them in. They put Dad in the squad car and Mom in an ambulance. I ride to the hospital with Mom because there's no one else at home. The cops come to the ER and ask Mom what exactly happened. And then they ask her if she wants to press charges.

She tells them, "No I don't want to press charges. We were arguing, and when I turned to walk away from him, he just grabbed my arm. It was my fault. I stumbled and fell. That's when I hit my head on the corner of the kitchen island." They seem satisfied with her story, and Dad is back home later that evening.

I'll never know if what Mom said is the truth about what happened that day. After that, there is no more yelling or hitting. They just file for divorce and go their separate ways. I'm relieved and happy that it will just be Mom, my sister, and me living together. Or so I thought.

# CHAPTER 16
# 2023

The week goes on, and I can't stop thinking about Amy. I wonder if she will ever have the courage to leave her abusive boyfriend. Seeing her bruised jaw has also brought up a lot of bad memories about my own childhood and my second marriage. I've been a little down, and by Thursday I decide to text Jordan. I go to my car on my lunch break, and after I eat my yogurt and blueberries, I take out my phone and think about what I want to say.

*Hey, Jordan. It's Kate. How's your week going? My week seems long, and I've been thinking a lot about last weekend. I had a lot of fun with you. Hope to see you again soon.*

I hit send and wait. I reread what I typed and dissect it in every way possible while I wait for a response. Ten minutes pass, and I begin to wonder if he's decided not to respond and that he's come to the conclusion that we shouldn't spend any more time together. I would be upset, but it would make my life easier, that's for sure. Just as I'm thinking about all sorts of scenarios, my phone chimes.

*Hi, Kate! It's good to hear from you. My week has been fine, a little busier at work than usual but good otherwise. I've been thinking about you too. A lot! I had the best time with you last weekend. When are you free to get together again?*

I read his message and I'm excited. Nope. Never mind. My life would not be easier if Jordan didn't want to see me. Just seeing his message makes my heart race and makes me happy. I only have a few minutes left on my lunch break, so I don't have much time to think about how to respond. But I need to let him know that I won't be able to spend time with him again for another week. So I just quickly type:

*That's very nice to hear. Unfortunately, I won't be free until a week from tomorrow. Will you be available the weekend of the 18th? Hope so!*

I think about saying more, but I decide to leave it at that. I've got to get back to work, so I silence my phone and put it in my purse. When I'm with patients, my purse is in the cabinet in my exam room, and I usually just check it a couple times a day to make sure I don't have any urgent messages. Noah isn't much of a texter, so I usually don't hear from him when I'm at work.

I take care of my 1:15 client, and my 2:15 is early, so I go right to that one next. By the time I'm done with both of them, it's 3:20 and my next appointment isn't until 3:45. I take my phone to our office break room and check my messages. Jordan responded to my last message seven minutes after I sent it.

*I understand. I will be free the weekend of the 18th and would love to see you. It actually works out great because I'm going to a baseball game with a couple of friends of mine this Saturday, and then I'm going to a car show with my best friend, Ben, on Sunday. Hope you have a great week, Kate. Already looking forward to seeing you next weekend!*

I'm literally shaking and smiling ear to ear when I read his message. Anna, the other hygienist in the office, walks into the break room and says, "Wow. Someone looks awfully happy."

I feel my cheeks turn red and I sputter out, "Huh, what?"

She says, "By that look on your face, it looks like your hubby messaged you something awfully naughty. Must be nice that you're still hot for each other like that after four years."

I bristle a little at the mention of Noah's name, but manage to smile and say, "Naughty? Not really. He's just romantic sometimes, that's all." I feel bad for lying to Anna. I really like her. She's in her late fifties, does not tolerate bullshit, and has a great, sarcastic sense of humor. At this point, if I was to confide in anyone about what's going on in my life, it would probably be her. But not now. Maybe not ever. I'm ashamed of what I'm doing, but not enough to put a stop to it. So I continue to lie.

I make a little small talk with Anna before she says, "Well, my 3:45 is here, and I'm just ecstatic about it. It's that guy who barely wears any cologne or hair gel." I laugh because there's her sarcastic humor that I love so much. The guy she's talking about douses himself in about a half a bottle of cologne and wears so much gel in his hair it could withstand a tornado without moving. We normally wouldn't say anything about a patient, but he's so obnoxious. He talks nonstop about how much weight he can lift at the gym and how many girls he's dating. She rolls her eyes, puts on her best fake smile, and walks out to the waiting room. I hear her cheerfully call out, "Matt, would you like to come on back?"

I'm still laughing as the strong smell of cologne wafts down the hall behind her. I pull out my phone and quickly send a message back:

**Have a great time with your friends this weekend! See you soon!**

I feel like that's enough said. I silence my phone and go back to take care of my last patient of the day. It's a fifteen-year-old who is terrified of the dentist. I do my best to convince her that I won't hurt her and take a little extra time doing her cleaning. By the time we're finished, she's smiling and says, "That didn't hurt at all. Can you take care of me when I come back in six months?" I tell her that I sure can.

When she goes out to the waiting room, her mom is waiting for her, and I hear her excitedly say, "Mom, it didn't hurt at all!" And this is exactly why I love my job.

# CHAPTER 17
# 2023

It's Friday. My day off. Noah is at work. I think about going to the market, but I decide it's not a good idea. I'm a little bummed that I'm not meeting up with Jordan today, but I know that I'll be seeing him soon, so it's not so bad.

I decide that I'm going to go to the pool in our subdivision. It's usually empty on Friday because most people are working, so it's typically the only day that I go down there. I lay on a lounge, put on my earbuds, and enjoy relaxing. When I get hot, I wade in the pool for a while and then return to my lounge. I'm shocked when I look at my watch and realize I've been there over three hours.

I go back home and shower. I'm about to start dinner when Noah calls and tells me not to bother because he's taking me out to dinner. Huh? I don't remember the last time he surprised me like this, and I can't help but wonder why he suddenly has the urge to take me out. I hadn't put any makeup on because I was at the pool, so I quickly do that and fix my hair by drying it and putting up in a ponytail. I'm not sure how to dress because I don't know where we're going, so I choose some black pants, a black shirt with silver thread running through it, and a pair of black wedge sandals. I put on my silver hoop earrings and wait for Noah to get home. I should be excited about a night out with my husband, but I only feel confused and conflicted.

He walks in with a bouquet of flowers for me, and I just about faint. Seriously. What's going on here? It's been at least a year since he brought me flowers. I suddenly have a sickening thought that he knows. Someone that knows us saw me, told him they saw me with another man, and now he's trying to be romantic. But why would he do that? Why wouldn't he just confront me? I scold myself. Stop it, Kate! If he thought you were with another man, the last thing he would do is bring you flowers!

But I'm still suspicious. "Wow. They're beautiful. Thanks. What's the occasion?"

He says, "Nothing. I was just thinking that after this I won't be here for the next few weekends, and I want to take you out and spend some time with you. And the flowers are just because you deserve something pretty once in a while." He hugs me and gives me a quick kiss. "Just give me a few minutes to walk Max and get changed. I'm taking you to your favorite Italian restaurant, the one on Dayton."

I'm pretty positive I'm standing there with my mouth still hanging open when he goes out the door with Max. We haven't gone to my favorite restaurant in forever. We've talked about going multiple times but never do. He's back from walking Max in record time and tells me he's going to shower, and he'll be ready to go in twenty minutes.

We drive to the restaurant, and Noah seems unusually happy and relaxed. I can't help but wonder where in the world this came from. Not that I don't believe him when he says he doesn't like being away from home for the next several weekends; it's just that usually it would just make him grouchy, and the last thing he would think of is taking me out when he's in a mood like that.

When we get to the restaurant, we don't have to wait because Noah apparently made a reservation for us. We get seated and he asks me, "Do you want to get a half bottle of wine, babe?" I'm taken aback again. He used to call me babe all the time when we first got together, but I haven't heard that in quite a while.

"Sure," I say. "That would be nice. How about a Pinot Noir?" He says that sounds great to him and orders it for us. We look over the menu. I decide on the veggie noodles with Bolognese sauce, and he orders the salmon with a side of pasta. The bread and wine have arrived, and we start eating.

"You look really pretty tonight, Kate," he says with a grin, and then he asks me how my day was.

I'm really surprised by him telling me I look pretty. I feel like it's been a long time since he looked at me like that. After a few seconds, I clear my throat and manage to respond. I tell him that he looks great too. I try to relax and tell him that my day was a lazy one—just hanging out at the pool and doing a little dusting and vacuuming. I ask him how his day was, and he tells me it was "fine." What the hell? I have never known him not to talk for at least fifteen minutes straight about every detail of his workday. My mind is whirling with all sorts of thoughts. What is going on here? He hasn't been this focused on me in forever, and it's making me, for lack of a better word, uncomfortable.

And then I start to feel very guilty and a little bit angry. I've pretty much felt invisible for more than a year, and I know that's a big reason that I starting talking to Jordan in the first place, so why now?! It's almost like he knows, but I'm sure he doesn't.

He interrupts my racing mind by saying, "Where'd you go? You look like you're zoned out. Oh, food is here." The waiter sets our plates down, and I suddenly don't feel like eating at all. I take a few bites and tell Noah I'm full.

"Was it okay? You sure didn't eat much."

"I think I ate too much bread. I'll take it home and put it in the freezer. I'll have it for lunch next week."

He pays the bill, we cork the remainder of the wine to take with us, and we head to the car.

Noah opens the car door for me, and it's just another thing that he hasn't done in forever. I'm becoming more and more suspicious of his behavior. I sound like a terrible person, but I can't just flip my mindset in one night. He's been distant and hasn't shown any romantic interest in me for such a long time that it almost feels wrong, like I'm with a stranger. And not in that exciting, first date kind of way. The only way I can explain it is that it feels weird, like someone who's been your friend forever suddenly tries to put the moves on you.

Now he says that it's such a beautiful night he wants to go to a drive-thru, get a cup of coffee, take a drive, and look at the stars. I can only manage to say, "Sure."

We get our coffee and drive around and talk for over an hour. I don't know how long he would have driven around if I hadn't been the one to say, "It's getting a little late. This has been great, but we should get home. We need to walk Max, and I need to take a load of clothes out of the dryer."

"Sure, babe, let's head home then." There's that "babe" again.

After we get home, he takes Max out and I fold the laundry. For once he doesn't want to sit on the couch with the dog and says he's ready to go to bed. We brush our teeth and get in bed. I thank him again for a great night, tell him how much I appreciate it, and lean over to give him a kiss. I get more than just a kiss. He gives me several kisses and then wants to wrap his arms around me when we lay down to go to sleep. I think if I didn't have about a million other thoughts running through my head, I might be happy that he's making some effort. But instead I just want it to end. I tell him I'm really tired, turn off the light, and roll away from him.

He puts his hand on my arm and says, "Goodnight, Kate. Love you."

I tell him I love him too. And then I silently cry myself to sleep.

***

He continues to be extra attentive all weekend and the rest of the week. He talks about work, but very little. And at night he makes Max lay on the floor instead of being wedged between us or in his lap on the couch. I'm having a hard time concentrating at work, and more than once I've thought about texting Jordan and telling him that I can't see him anymore. But that thought makes my heart ache, and I can't seem to make myself do it. I'm grateful when Thursday finally comes. Noah will be going to the airport in the afternoon to head out for the first of his several weekends of working out of town.

On Wednesday afternoon, I had texted Jordan and asked him what he wanted to do this weekend. He asked me if I wanted to see a movie Friday, and I said that I'd like that. But now I'm a little worried that someone I know might see me. It's like he can read my mind because the next day he texted me to let me know that the theater we're going to is in a town that's about thirty minutes from where we live. I silently thank him for not making me bring up the fact that I don't want to take the risk of running into someone I know.

I keep telling myself that what I'm doing is okay. I mean, sure, I'm attracted to Jordan, but all we've been doing is hanging out together. There's nothing physical going on. I guess I think if I keep telling myself that, I will become convinced that there's nothing wrong with what I'm doing. If there's nothing wrong with it, then why do I feel so guilty? Shut up, conscience, shut up!

When I get home from work Thursday night, I feel absolutely exhausted. My emotions have been all over the place, and it has worn me out. Noah calls just as I'm heading off to bed, and it's a very short conversation. There's no "babe" this time. He tells me he made it to Florida and he's really tired. He says he's going to order room service and then go to bed. I hear all kinds of noise in the background, and he says he's in the hotel bar having a drink. He tells me that he's not sure if I'll hear from him much over the weekend. It's three hours later there, and he doesn't want to wake me up if he gets done with work late. I tell him that's fine and I understand. He's flying back late Sunday night, and then he'll have Monday and Tuesday off because of working all weekend. I tell him to sleep well.

"Goodnight," he says, then hangs up. He seems irritated, and I get it. Flying all evening and having to be in a strange place all alone isn't any fun.

My phone rings right after we hang up, and I think that it's Noah calling me back, but it's my sister, Morgan. She's calling to tell me that Mom is upset because our stepdad went on a bender last weekend and didn't come home for two days.

"What else is new, Morgan?" Mom and I barely talk to each other, and we have a very contentious relationship. She talks to Morgan pretty often, so that's how I know what's going on. It's not that I really want or need to talk to her anymore. I stopped trying to be mom's cheerleader/caregiver a long time ago.

# CHAPTER 18
# 1992

Once the divorce is final, Mom, Morgan, and I move into a tiny apartment in a crummy part of town. Morgan and I don't care about leaving our big house, where we had separate bedrooms, and sharing one tiny bedroom. We're just so happy to get away from all the fighting and violence that we've been living in for the past few years.

We also think that we will get our mom back. She has to work now, which she has not done since she and our dad first got married, so she won't have much time for her "party girl" ways anymore. Mom never went to college, but she is smart and very personable. She has two job offers right away—one is a secretary for a real estate office and the other is driving the courtesy shuttle for a car dealership.

For some reason she turns both of those offers down and takes a job as a maid at a local motel. I know now that it was because she was scared that she would fail and decided to stick to something she knew well—cleaning. She'd been cleaning up after a husband and three kids for the past twenty-one years.

She starts her job at the motel a couple of weeks before we have to move out of our house, and sometimes she works weekends and sometimes just Monday through Friday; her schedule varies every month. She has to be there at six in the morning, but she's done and home before three so she can pick us up from school. A neighbor from our old neighborhood offers to drive us to school on the weekday mornings that Mom works, since my sister and I are friends with her daughters.

We move into our new apartment on a Saturday morning. Mom worked all week and has the weekend off. We don't have a lot except for our beds and a couple of dressers. Dad buys us some furniture, a television, some dishes, a toaster, and a coffee maker. That's Dad's way—I beat you up and screamed at you for years, so here's a coffee maker.

We get mostly unpacked and Mom orders pizza for our first night. Morgan and I are giddy to say the least. It feels like a slumber party, and we know that no one is going to be screaming or throwing things. It's close to ten now, but Mom doesn't make us go to bed. She's never let me stay up this late. She keeps looking out the front window, and we start to wonder what's going on. Is that bitch Jane coming to pick her up so they can go out drinking?

A little after ten, mom leaps out of her chair, goes into the bathroom, and puts on more lipstick. Morgan and I jump because someone is pounding on the door. Mom comes running out of the bathroom with a big smile on her face and opens the door. There is a man standing there that I've never seen before. He's carrying a suitcase. Why is he carrying a suitcase? Mom turns to us and says, "Girls, this is Ron. He's my boyfriend, and he's going to live with us!" She is beyond excited, and Morgan and I are in total shock.

Ron is obviously drunk, swaying back and forth and slurring his words. He says to Mom, "I hope this works. I really don't like kids." Mom assures him that we are good and won't bother him. Morgan and I both start to cry, and Mom tells us to stop it right now and go to bed.

My sister and I go to our tiny room and get in our beds. I'm still crying, and Morgan is telling me that it's going to be okay. But I can tell by the fear in her voice that she doesn't believe that. The walls in the apartment are thin, so we are whispering to each other. I ask Morgan if she ever saw Ron before. She says that she thinks she saw him once when Mom came home late one night after going out drinking.

"This was last year," she says. "Dad was working out of town. You had fallen asleep on the couch, but I was scared to go to sleep because we were home alone. I kept looking out the window, waiting for Mom to come home. It was after midnight, and I saw a car I didn't recognize pull in the driveway. Mom got out of the passenger side, and this guy got out to help her to the front door. They stood at the front door kissing for a long time before Mom finally came in. It was dark, but I'm pretty sure it was this guy."

Mom and Ron are not aware or just don't care that the walls are thin. We can clearly hear them talking and laughing. Then we have to hear them having sex. Loudly. And it is beyond traumatic.

***

The next morning Morgan and I get up and try to be quiet. We get ourselves some cereal and turn the television on but keep the volume low. Mom finally comes out of her bedroom a little after nine, and she's grinning from ear to ear. She practically sings "Good morning!" to us.

Morgan says, "Mom, who is this guy? And what do you mean he's going to live with us? We don't want him here!" Mom's stupid grin disappears immediately, and she looks really mad. She tells us that we need to behave and let her be happy. Then she tries to tell us that Ron is so great and we'll all have a great time living together.

Before anything else can be said, Ron comes out of the bedroom. In his underwear. Mom runs over to him, throws her arms around him, and asks what he'd like for breakfast. She's acting like a sixteen-year-old, and it's nauseating.

"You can just make me some bacon and eggs, and then I've got to go," he says. Mom obediently makes his breakfast and practically sits in his lap while he eats. He hasn't even acknowledged that my sister and I are in the room.

After he's done with breakfast, Mom asks him where he's going and when he'll be back. He tells her it's none of her business, and if she's going to act like his mother, then he'll just move back in with his cousin.

Morgan and I look at each other, and our faces both say 'Good! Move back in with your cousin!' Our smirks turn to giggling, and Ron is angry now. Mom tells us to stop and Morgan says, "Why? All we're doing is laughing."

Ron tells Mom that we're brats, grabs his jacket, and leaves. When she's sure he's out of earshot, Morgan yells out "Good riddance!" and we both start laughing again. Mom bursts into tears and tells us we are ruining her life. She spends most of the day crying on and off while she finishes unpacking. She gives us peanut butter and jelly sandwiches for dinner, but she doesn't eat all day.

She finally smiles again when Ron comes staggering through the door after eleven o'clock that night. My sister and I are devastated that he's come back, and we know that from this point forward our lives are never going to be the same.

# CHAPTER 19
# 2023

Jordan and I have decided to meet in the parking lot of the organic market and drive to the movie theater from there. I decide on jeans, a blue sleeveless top, and my favorite wedge sandals. I bring a jacket too because the theater is usually cold. I'm a mix of emotions when the time comes to drive to the market. On one hand I'm excited to see Jordan, but on the other hand, Noah and I had a great time before he left. The feeling of guilt is overpowering my anticipation.

When I pull into the parking lot, Jordan is already there, and my heartbeat quickens when I see his car. I get out, and he gets out of his car too. He walks to me and looks so happy to see me.

"Hi, Kate. Wow, you look beautiful tonight." I say thank you and tell him he looks great too. And he really does. He's got on some dark-washed jeans with a light gray short-sleeve shirt. Sounds like nothing special, but he has a knack for choosing clothes that flatter his dark skin and fit him perfectly. He smells fantastic too. He's wearing just a hint of good cologne.

I'm surprised when he hugs me, and I'm even more surprised when he says, "You smell so good. I like your perfume." Funny that I was thinking how good his cologne smells and then he mentions my perfume. That guilty feeling is going away rapidly, and now I feel like I'm just happy to see my friend. But the thoughts I've had about this man are definitely *not* thoughts you'd have about someone who is just your friend.

My internal battle is interrupted by him speaking. "All ready to go?" We get in his car and drive to the theater in the next town. Conversation flows easily while we drive, and it doesn't seem like any time at all before we're at the theater.

There are a few good choices, and Jordan asks me what I'd like to see—Romance? Horror? Action? I ask him what he prefers, and he says he'll let me pick this time and he'll pick next time. Fair. I choose the action movie, and he says he's a bit surprised.

"You were sure I was going to pick the romantic comedy, weren't you?"

He admits that was exactly what he thought and then says, "You continue to surprise me, Kate, and I like that. And excellent choice on the movie. I really wanted to see that one."

We go in and take our seats. We sit in the very back of the theater, which was also my pick. I hate people sitting behind me in a movie theater. The theater was a perfect choice for tonight. I love talking to him, but it will be nice to get lost in a movie and not have to talk for a couple of hours.

The movie is good; we're both enjoying it. We have our arms touching on the arm rest for the entire movie, and it does not go unnoticed by me. There's a scene where a female undercover agent does a striptease for the male lead character, and, of course, she ends up dancing around topless.

Jordan turns to me and whispers, "What a surprise. Not only is she topless, but all female undercover agents look like supermodels!" I nod in agreement and we both laugh. There's that sense of humor that I love, and it helps to make watching the scene with him, which seems really long, a little less awkward.

We leave the movie and head out to the parking lot. "I was thinking we could get a cup of coffee, if you'd like," Jordan suggests. I tell him that sounds nice and we find a cute little place close to the theater.

We sit down and order our coffee. He asks me how work was last week, and I ask him how his car show and baseball game were last weekend. Conversation flows easily, like it has every time we've been together, and time goes by fast. "I'm having a great time," he says. "But we should head back soon. It's after eleven o'clock." I can't believe it. Did he just say after eleven? Time really did fly by!

When we get back to the parking lot, he walks me to my car, and I'm not sure what to say at this point. Is this it for the weekend, or does he want to see me Saturday or Sunday? I decide to leave the ball in his court. I thank him for the movie and tell him what a great time I had. He opens my door for me, and I'm thinking that must be it, so I get in and put my seatbelt on.

He surprises me by saying, "I'm going to see you tomorrow, aren't I?"

"Sure. What do you have in mind?"

He hesitates for a few seconds and then says, "Um, how would you feel about coming to my place? I'd like to cook you a steak." It's my turn to hesitate for a few seconds. I'd never considered us being together outside of a public place, and I'm a little taken aback.

I ultimately decide that offer sounds really good, and I say, "Yes, that sounds great."

"Great! I live on Rosalinda Road. I'll text you the address tomorrow. Does six o'clock work for you?"

"Sure," I nod. "Sounds good." I push the ignition button and start up the car, looking up at his blue eyes again as the engine roars to life. "See you tomorrow. Goodnight, Jordan." I smile. He tells me goodnight, gets in his car, and waits until I've pulled out before he starts his car.

I take out my phone at the first stoplight I come to and see that I have a text from Noah. My heart starts to pound. What time did he send it? Is he upset that I didn't respond? The light turns green, and I have to put the phone down. At the next red light, I look at Noah's message again.

*Hey. I know you won't see this until tomorrow morning. I had a very long day and then had dinner with one of the territory managers. I'm heading to bed now.*

I see that the message was sent at 10:42 my time, so it wasn't that long ago. I pull over into a parking lot and send a reply. I say that I had dozed off with the television on and just woke up and saw his message. I tell him goodnight and that I'll try to call him tomorrow. If he was still up at almost two in the morning Florida time, he must be working his butt off. And just like that, the sickening feeling of guilt has returned.

***

I sleep unusually late the next morning and don't get up until about 7:45. I take Max for a long walk and then have some yogurt and toast for breakfast.

I'm trying to decide if I should work out or not. I did walk at least three miles with Max this morning, but I should do some weight training. I'm dedicated to my workouts, but sometimes people give me a hard time about it. I wouldn't criticize someone for choosing not to work out, so I'm not sure why they feel like it's okay to judge someone who does. The list of comments is endless, but my favorites are: "Why do you even work out at all? You're so skinny!" "Come on, Kate. Would it kill you to have a donut with us once in a while?" "You know age is going to catch up with you one of these days, and all this working out will be for nothing."

I'm not skinny. I'm a normal, healthy weight, and I want to stay that way. They don't know about my struggles with weight in the past and that, to this day, I can gain weight very easily if I'm not vigilant about my diet and exercise. I vowed to never be obese again, and I have successfully maintained a healthy weight since I was seventeen, except for a few times in my twenties when I was going through hard times and lost too much weight. The way I lost the weight initially was not healthy at all, and now I keep it off the healthy way. The right way.

# CHAPTER 20
# 2000

I'm sixteen and want to start dating and enjoying the things that it seems like all the other girls in high school are doing. I have my driver's license, and Dad just bought me a used car. Of course he bought it for me because the last time he saw me, which was quite a while ago, he screamed at me—this time in a public place.

He asked me to meet him for lunch because he has some money for me to give to Mom and he said he'd like to see me. He's never paid child support through the court system. He and my mom agreed on him paying her with a personal check from the beginning. Sometimes he doesn't want to mail it because he's paying it on the last day of the month, and he really doesn't want to go to Mom's house because of Ron. So, a lot of times, I'm the go-between.

Mom dropped me off at the restaurant, and as soon as I walked over to the table, I could tell he was mad. He was upset because I dyed my light-brown hair bright red. He was seeing it for the first time, and I could tell I was about to get yelled at.

We were in public, and I didn't want a scene, so I tried to sound happy and said, "Hi, Dad. I've missed you."

He didn't even say hi to me. He just shouted, "What did you do to your hair? It looks terrible on you! What in the hell was your mother thinking letting you do that to yourself?!"

I quietly said, "What's the big deal, Dad? It's just hair."

Then, of course, he told me it looked even worse on me because I was fat and looked bad enough as it is. There were several people around, and I was so embarrassed. I didn't respond at all, not a single word. I just wordlessly got up, walked out of the restaurant, and walked all the way back home.

No more than a week later, he called Mom to let her know that he bought me a car. I was still so hurt and mad that I refused to see him, so he ended up just dropping the car off for me.

Shortly after the incident with my father, I'm in my high school English class and the assignment for the day is that we all have to get up in front of the class and read our papers out loud. I'm one of the last ones to get up because I sit in the very back of the class. I hate getting up in front of anyone, but I especially hate getting up in front of the class, and I'm shaking as I read my paper.

When I finish I start walking back to my seat, but before I can sit down, a boy who is always bullying me moos like a cow loudly. All the kids in the class start laughing, and I feel like I want to die. The teacher tells him that he's just earned detention. She tells him to go to the office and have the principal call his parents to let them know he will have to stay after school an hour each day for a week, starting today. He's still laughing when he walks out of the classroom and seems completely unfazed. She warns the rest of the class to stop laughing or they'll all get detention too. Again, I wish the ground would open up and swallow me.

I go home and resolve to lose the sixty extra pounds I'm carrying. I want to do it fast, so I come up with a plan to just eat one banana a day and to drink only water. I vow to do this until I lose all the weight. At sixteen years old, I don't realize how dangerous and stupid my plan is, especially given my medical history. I don't tell anyone what I'm doing, eat one last big dinner that night, and start my plan the next day.

I get up the following morning and eat my banana, but nothing else for the rest of the day. I'm so hungry and almost give in and eat something, but I just keep drinking water to try to feel full. I manage to do this for an entire week, and after seven days I step on the scale. I'm shocked to see that I have already lost nine pounds. This is all the motivation I need to keep going. After I lose about twenty-five pounds, people start to notice and tell me how great I look.

I become an expert at pushing my food around on my plate to make it look like I'm eating at least some of my dinner. Mom just thinks I'm losing weight because I'm eating less and not drinking soda anymore. I manage to lose all sixty pounds in just under two months, but I don't want to quit. I decide to go for ten more, then ten more, then ten more. I spend my weekends babysitting for our neighbors and use all of the money I earn to buy new clothes.

Mom can tell I'm losing weight, but she has no idea just how much. I start wearing loose, baggy clothes so people can't tell how thin I've become, now down ninety pounds. When Mom and Ron go to bed at night, I get up and, in the dark, do jumping jacks and sit ups for at least an hour every night. Now I'm at least twenty-five pounds underweight, and I don't know how to stop doing what I'm doing. I'm terrified if I start to eat normally again, I'll gain all the weight back.

Mom finally figures it out one day when she catches me wearing a pair of shorts and a T-shirt while I'm hanging out in my room. I think she's at work, so I take a shower and get dressed in my size zero clothes, which are hanging loosely on my bony frame. Mom walks into my room unannounced to put some laundry away and is shocked at my gaunt appearance. She tells me that I'd better start eating or she is going to call my dad and tell him how skinny I am.

Way to go, Mom—don't ask me what would make me do this to myself or offer to help me, just try to scare me into gaining weight. I hadn't seen my dad since he screamed at me in public, and she knows that's the only threat that really scares me. I agree that I will start eating a little more and beg her not to call Dad.

It takes me a long time to get back to a normal weight, and I will struggle for the rest of my life with a bad body image, sometimes even reverting to depriving myself of food. It's not until I start going to counseling that this destructive pattern finally stops.

I start to eat a little more, and I do gain about fifteen pounds back. I finally feel like I'm ready to show Dad that I lost weight, which is what he's wanted me to do for years. I call him, and he sounds like he's genuinely happy to hear from me. He says he feels bad about what happened the last time he saw me and to come on over. I put on a pair of jeans and a T-shirt and head over to Dad's house. I knock on his door, and as I'm standing there, I'm smiling, thinking that he will finally tell me he's proud of me.

When he opens the door, he looks at me for a few seconds like he doesn't even know who I am. Then he finally says, "Oh my. What have you done?"

"I did what you always wanted me to do, Dad. I went on a diet. How do I look?"

He furrows his brow and says, "Well, I don't think you look good. You're way too thin now."

Are you kidding me?! That's when I know. No matter what I do in my life, I will never be able to make him happy. He's always going to think that my sisters can do no wrong and that I am the perpetual disappointment. Straight A's, losing weight, getting awards at school…none of it will ever get him to be proud of me. From that day forward, he and I barely have any relationship at all and will sometimes go months without seeing or talking to each other.

***

When I'm twenty-nine, I will get a call from my oldest sister, Jessica, telling me that Dad died from a massive heart attack. I will cry at his funeral, but I really won't be that upset. My biggest concern will be if Gail will show up at the funeral. She will have dumped my dad years ago, when I was fifteen, which I will have been ecstatic about, but I don't think Dad will have ever stopped hoping she would take him back. I won't know what happened to her after that, and I won't care, but it would be just like her to have the nerve to show up. I will be watching the door because I will have decided that if she walks in, I'm going to tell her she's not welcome and to get out. She won't show up, and I'll actually be a little disappointed. I will no longer be that overweight little girl that she verbally abused, and I would be looking forward to finally telling her off.

After Dad's gone I won't miss him at all, and I will never go to visit his grave. By the time Dad passes away, Mom and I won't have much of a relationship with each other. I will feel very alone.

# CHAPTER 21
# 2023

After I do about a half hour of weight lifting, I shower and put on my makeup. I'm as nervous about tonight as I was the first time I decided to "accidentally" run into Jordan at the market. Maybe more! I decide on pair of capri pants, a fitted black shirt, and sandals. After I get dressed, I take Max out for a quick walk and text Jordan to get his address. He responds right away:

*Hi, Kate! The address is 33945 Rosalinda Road. My neighborhood is gated so you will have to put in the code. It's 0605#. If you have any trouble with gate, just text me. When you get here, one of the garage stalls will be open, so go ahead and pull your car in. See you around 6:00!*

Again, he's thinking ahead more than I am. I wouldn't want anyone I know to see my car parked in his driveway, and I'm sure that's why he offered to let me park it in his garage. I mapped Jordan's neighborhood earlier in the day, and it's only about ten minutes from my house, so I grab my purse and a bottle of wine and head out the door right at 5:50. When I get to the gate, I punch in the code, and it slides right open for me. I pull into one of the three stalls of his garage and knock on the door that leads from the garage into the house.

When he opens the door, I'm even more overcome with nervousness. I'm about to go in his house, and this feels more intimate and personal than any of the other times we've seen each other. It must be written all over my face because he says, "Hi. Are you alright?" I assure him that I'm fine, and he says, "Come in, please come in."

I hand him the bottle of Cabernet that I brought, and he tells me that I didn't need to bring anything but we will open it and have a glass with dinner. "Do you want a quick tour of the house?"

"I would love that," I nod.

He takes me through the kitchen first, which is very beautiful. He's a minimalist, and I like it. Most of the walls are painted white, but he has a couple of accent walls that are done in dark colors or with reclaimed wood. The kitchen has a big, beautiful island and chef-quality appliances. There is a primary bedroom and three additional bedrooms, one that he's made into a gym and another he's designed as a den that he uses for his office. There are also three bathrooms.

The house is a single story, and even though everything in it looks pretty high end, it's not over-the-top fancy. I'm guessing it's about 2,500 square feet. The floors are all hardwood or tile, but he has big area rugs in all the bedrooms and the living room, which makes those spaces feel warm and inviting. I like how he's decorated, and I feel like it's very similar to the house I lived in before I moved into Noah's place, with the exception being that my house was about half this size. He's got soft, instrumental music playing at a perfect low volume, and it's helping me to relax.

When I've seen everything, I say, "You've got a beautiful place Jordan. It's really warm, and I like how you've decorated." I'm standing next to his stove and ask, "Do you like to cook and entertain a lot?"

"Thank you so much. I can't take all the credit for choosing the décor, but I appreciate the compliment." I'm sure that his late wife did most of the decorating, but I don't want to ask and risk bringing up anything that's going to upset him. He leans against the counter and says, "I love to cook, and I have a couple people over for dinner from time to time." He smiles at me and adds, "I have a very small circle of friends." I smile back. Good answer.

He tells me that he has some potatoes with asparagus and mushrooms in the oven and he's about ready to start the steaks if I'm ready. "Oops," he quickly adds. "I guess I should have asked you if you like those veggies first. Sorry."

"No worries—I love them. I'm not very picky." He smiles and turns his attention to the stove.

"Would you mind opening the wine and pouring us a taste?" He gets down a couple of stemless wine glasses for me, and I pour us a small sample. He picks up his glass and walks over close to me. "Cheers, Kate, I'm so glad you're here."

"Me too. Cheers." We clink our glasses together and sip the wine. It's smooth and not overly dry. I'm relieved that I chose a great bottle.

"Wow. That's excellent. Thanks again for bringing it." I ask him if he needs help with anything, but he says, "Not at all, but you know what you can do for me? How about you make yourself comfortable? Take a seat here at the island and just let me take care of you."

"I will try to resist the urge to help," I laugh as I take a seat. I pour both of us more wine and watch him cook. He sears our steaks on the stovetop, then puts them in the oven to finishing cooking, and everything smells just amazing! He leans against the island next to me and asks me how my day was.

"It was pretty routine," I reply as I take a sip of wine. "How was yours?"

"Same. Time seemed to move very slowly because I couldn't wait to see you tonight."

I blush. "I felt the same way."

We make some small talk while dinner finishes cooking and then move over to his dining room table. He tells me to please just sit and let him serve me. He has chosen filet mignons for tonight, obviously because I said it's my favorite cut, and puts a perfectly cooked (medium) steak on my plate with a generous spoonful of the veggies on the side. After he fills his own plate, he dims the lights and lights a couple of candles that are on the table. Between the smell of the steaks, the music, and the lighting, I feel like I'm in a fancy steakhouse.

He looks a little nervous and says, "I hope it's good. Please let me know if it's not cooked the way you like it."

I take a bite and it's beyond good. It's amazing! I close my eyes and relish the flavor. "I know you'll probably think I'm exaggerating, but this is heavenly. It's as good as anything I've had in an expensive steakhouse. Great job, Jordan!"

He gives me a huge smile and says, "Really? I'm not sure it's that good, but I'm so glad that you like it."

Then he takes a bite, and I say, "Well?" He admits that it's pretty darn good and we enjoy the rest of our dinner. I eat every last bite, and he is so happy that I enjoyed it.

He loads the dishes into the dishwasher, again not letting me help, and pours us more wine. He sits down across from me again, and we are both suddenly shy and at a loss for words.

Jordan starts, "I don't want to bring down the mood, but I feel like I need to tell you something." My heart starts to race. Is he going to tell me that we can't see each other anymore? I know that we shouldn't be seeing each other to begin with, but I'm just not ready to face ending this right now.

I finally take a breath and say, "I'm listening. What do you want to tell me?"

He exhales sharply. "Here's the thing: I'm starting to have feelings for you, Kate, and I know that it's inappropriate and it's wrong, but I can't help how I feel. The very first time I saw you, I felt some sort of instant connection to you, and the only other time I've experienced anything like that in my life was with my wife, Rachel. It only took a couple of dates for me to know that I was in love with her and she felt the same way about me. I keep telling myself that I should do the smart thing and stop seeing you, but I can't, I just can't." He shakes his head before continuing.

"Then the guilt is overwhelming because you're married, and I know that what we're doing is wrong. I guess what I'm getting at is that I don't know what's going to happen here, but in a very short time, you've become very important to me."

His voice wavers with emotion on those last few words, and I'm just looking at him completely stunned by what he's just said. He's looking at me almost like he's pleading for me to respond. And I finally do.

"Jordan, I want you to know that I feel exactly what you're feeling. And the conflict that goes on inside me because of it makes me want to stop seeing you, but I just can't. I somehow feel inexplicably drawn to you, and I knew it the very first time I saw you in that grocery store. And I know what you're saying about the guilt, but I don't want to stop seeing you either. I can't give you any answers about what's going to happen with us, but I just know that I feel more alive than I've felt in a long time, and I don't want it to end."

When I'm finally done talking, Jordan gets up from the table, walks over to me and extends his hand. "Come here," he says. I stand up and take his hand, and he immediately pulls me in for a long hug. Our bodies are pressed tightly together for the first time, and I'm absolutely weak with desire for him. He strokes my hair and my back and I'm wishing it would never end. After what seems like a very long time, we finally release each other and we both sigh. I know it's a sigh of relief because we finally got the "what is this between us and what in the hell are we doing?" conversation over with.

We sit back down at the table, and I'm surprised again when he says, "I'd like to tell you about Rachel, if that's okay with you."

"I'd love to hear about her."

He smiles at my response. "We met right before I finished college. She was in her first year pursuing a teaching degree, and I was finishing up my degree in business. I was so focused on school that I didn't date much and didn't really have a lot of friends that I hung out with. One night a buddy of mine from one of my classes asked me if I wanted to go grab dinner at a restaurant around the corner from where I lived. I had a small apartment that I shared with two roommates who were never there because they both had girlfriends. I thought, what the heck, I could stand a night out for once.

"Rachel was working nights as a waitress at the restaurant, and we got sat in her section. Literally the moment she brought us our menus and I looked at her the first time, I couldn't take my eyes off her. And it wasn't just because she was beautiful, I felt drawn to her. When she brought us our check, I asked for her phone number, and a year later I asked her to marry me. We got married when I was thirty and she was twenty-seven. She wanted to wait until she was done with school and we were both well established in our careers. I would have married her the day after she said yes, but I respected what she wanted and it made sense.

"She was beautiful, smart, and had a fantastic sense of humor. She treated me like a king, and I think I treated her like a queen. We were head over heels in love, and I never got tired of looking at her. And we always had a hard time keeping our hands off each other." He had been smiling the whole time he was telling me about Rachel, but he suddenly began to look very sad.

"We had only been married a little over a year. One evening I was at home working in the garage, putting some stain on a bench that I was refinishing for her. Rachel loved to find old, beat-up furniture and have me try to bring it back to life."

"It was a little after eight when I got the call from the police asking me to come to the hospital because Rachel had been involved in an accident. She had been out having dinner with her best friend, who lived about twenty minutes away from us, and was heading home. She had just pulled onto the highway when a car crossed the center line and ran into her head on. Rachel was killed instantly. The driver of the other car was only twenty years old and walked away with a broken arm and a gash on his forehead. Turns out he was texting his girlfriend while he was driving and that's what caused him to veer into Rachel's lane. He got sentenced to forty-five years in prison and will probably only end up serving half of that, which isn't nearly long enough in my opinion, and the only solace I have is that Rachel was killed instantly."

"I know that it sounds strange that I'm comforted by that, but at least I know she wasn't in any pain and I didn't have to watch her lay in some hospital bed and die. The hardest thing I ever had to do in my life was go and identify her body, and I don't wish that on my very worst enemy."

Jordan now has tears in his eyes and I'm full-blown crying. "I'm so sorry. I shouldn't have talked about that," he says.

I take his hand in mine. "Don't be sorry at all. I'm glad you told me about Rachel. She sounds like she was a fantastic person and wife, and I can't tell you how sorry I am about what happened to her. Life can be so unfair sometimes."

He looks relieved and asks, "Would you like to see a picture of her?"

"I would like that very much." He gets up from the table and goes to his bedroom. He returns with a small, framed picture of her. She was an absolute beauty. Dark hair, dark eyes, and a smile that could light up a room. "Oh, Jordan, she was really beautiful. And what a smile. Wow."

"Thanks, Kate. Yeah, she was even more beautiful on the inside." He takes a last look at the picture and then takes it back to the bedroom. When he returns he says, "I'd like for you to tell me about Noah." I stiffen at the mention of Noah's name, and a wave of guilt washes over me.

I don't want to go into a lot of detail, so I tell him about how Noah and I met online in 2019 and got married in 2020. "He's a good man. In fact, he's a great man. He works hard and makes sure I have everything I need. He has a great sense of humor, although I haven't seen much of that side of him lately. And when we first got married, he was really romantic and did things like bring me flowers and plan date nights, but romance has almost become nonexistent in the past year.

"He's pretty obsessed with work, and I try not to complain about it because I'm proud of how hard he works and what he's accomplished. It's just that sometimes it's a bit much for me—always traveling, on his phone, or on his computer. Seems like we can never even sit down to dinner without work interrupting. And…"

I hesitate, and Jordan says, "What is it, Kate?"

"I feel bad saying this because he really is a great guy, but here goes. I told you before that there's been a lack of romance lately, but to be honest, there's no intimacy in our marriage at all. It just gradually decreased and has been completely nonexistent for the past several months now. I tried to initiate it for a long time, but he was always too tired or had some other excuse so I just stopped. There was one night recently that he took me by surprise and wanted to kiss me, but I really felt nothing and I stopped it.

"I feel like a terrible person for how I feel, and I think it's just because we've been in a dry spell for so long, but it has me worried that we'll never get those feelings back again." I pause and then add, "And I'm not sure I want to get them back."

"I'm sorry that you feel like that. Sure, intimacy waxes and wanes during a marriage, but it should never disappear completely. You aren't getting what you need, Kate, and it's okay for you to be upset about that. Other than that it sounds like he's a good guy though, right?"

"Yes, Noah is a great guy, and I do love him. He doesn't abuse me or treat me badly in any way, but I just don't feel like I'm completely happy in the marriage anymore. I feel ignored and unseen, and I sure as hell don't feel attractive anymore. But I feel so guilty for having those feelings because, after all, he's working his butt off to make an even better life for us, you know?"

"Stop right there. I've told you before and I'll tell you a million times more if I have to. You are beautiful, Kate, and really, really sexy. And he should be telling you that every single day and showing you how he feels, no matter how much work gets in the way or how tired he is."

He stops talking and looks embarrassed. Then he says, "I'll admit that I've had thoughts about how much I'd like to kiss you, hold you, touch you—" He stops quickly. "Sorry, I shouldn't have said that, but I want you to realize that you are just plain hot!"

We both start laughing, which is good because I didn't know how to respond to what he just said. "Hot, huh? All right, I'll take that."

I know he's trying to change the subject when he says, "So you didn't marry Noah until 2020 right? Was that your first marriage?" I cringe at his question and think carefully about how I want to answer it. Will he be completely turned off by the fact that Noah is my third husband? Will it make him think less of me as a person? I take a deep breath before answering.

"I was married before Noah. Twice." Jordan looks a little surprised, but I go on and say, "The first time I got married, I was only eighteen and I wasn't in love with the guy and he wasn't in love with me. We got married to escape our dysfunctional home lives, which was not a good reason. We had nothing in common and struggled through four years of marriage before getting divorced.

"From there I went pretty much directly to husband number two. I was scared because I was alone for the first time in my life and I didn't know if I could do it by myself, so I married him even though I knew I shouldn't. He was abusive, and after a very violent incident, which I don't want to talk about, I filed for divorce after less than a year of marriage.

"I had one long-term relationship after that, and aside from a disastrous six-month relationship, when I met Noah, I'd been single for almost five years. I swore I'd never get married again, but after we'd been together for more than a year, we decided it was what we both wanted. So here we are. I'm not proud of some of the choices I made in the past, and I hope you don't think less of me."

I hold my breath while I wait for him to respond. "I'm actually surprised by what you just told me, but, Kate, I can't believe you thought I would think less of you. If anything I'm even more impressed by you. Sounds like you endured some pretty rough stuff and you were able to pick yourself up, dust yourself off, and start over again and again, and that's no small feat. Anyone who sits in judgment of you doesn't know about your circumstances, so screw them!"

I can't believe that this guy is for real, and I'm feeling like I just unloaded a thousand-pound weight I've been carrying around. Noah has never judged me for my past either, but he does make jokes about it—not ever about the abusive relationships I've had, just the fact that I seem to have been a magnet for losers. Sometimes that hurts more than he knows.

"You don't know how much that means to me, Jordan. I feel like I've been judged more on my mistakes than my accomplishments my whole life, so thank you."

"I've got to ask. You told me that you lost your dad when you were twenty-nine and your stepdad is kind of a piece of work, but what about your mom? And I remember you telling me that you have two sisters. Didn't any of them try to help you and support you when you were going through all those tough times?"

I offer a weak smile and shake of my head. "No. In Jessica's defense, she's thirteen years older than me, so we've never been close at all, and as far as Morgan and my mother go, well, that's a story for another day…"

# CHAPTER 22
# 1994

I'm ten years old, and Morgan is fifteen. We have just moved into a tiny house on the other side of town. Much to my sister's and my dismay, Ron is still in the picture. We had so hoped he'd be long gone by now, but here he is, moving into the house with us and Mom.

He works at one of those ten-minute oil change places, and come Friday night, every Friday night, he starts drinking the minute he's done at work and doesn't stop until Sunday morning. He's been there quite a while and works until eight on Friday nights, so he almost never has to work on Saturday. He rarely comes home on the weekends, has had numerous affairs, and has been arrested for drunk driving a couple of times.

And there's Mom. Constantly defending him and just letting him use her whenever he feels like it. She thinks she could never make it on her own and that she needs Ron. I never understood that because Ron spends most of his check on booze and who knows what else. We sometimes don't have any food in the house, and our electricity and phone get shut off pretty often. A lot of times, my dad has to pay our bills or bring us groceries.

Morgan is starting to stay away from home and hang out with her friends as much as possible, so that leaves me there alone with Mom and Ron. I always hope he won't come home on the weekends, and he usually doesn't, but I still don't get any time with Mom because she spends the whole weekend crying and pining for Ron.

When he is there, he makes it clear that I'm not to be seen or heard, and he doesn't like the fact that I'm getting older and starting to talk back. I'm grounded pretty frequently and spend a fair amount of my life in my bedroom. When Ron is home, Mom acts like a fourteen-year-old girl with a crush. She's stuck to him like glue and they completely ignore me. The only time I really have anyone to talk to is when Morgan is home, and that's not very often.

***

In 1996 everyone, especially Morgan and I, is shocked when Mom and Ron announce that they are getting married. We can't come up with one reason why Ron would agree to marry my mom after being able to just use her whenever he feels like it for the past four years. It doesn't make any sense to us.

Years later we would find out that Ron thought he was going to get his hands on some money. Turns out that our dad had a separate bank account with $50,000 in it and had designated Mom to be the beneficiary of it in his will. It specified that Mom was to use that money to take care of Morgan and me if we were still minors and that if we were over eighteen when he passed away, the money was to automatically go to me, Morgan, and Jessica and be split between us three ways.

Ron had no idea that the deal was null and void if Mom remarried or that Jessica, Morgan, and I were already designated to get the money if we were over eighteen at the time of Dad's death. Mom knew this but never told Ron, and she pretended to be shocked about it when Dad died. If Morgan and I would have known anything about it, we would have told Ron. We're pretty positive he wouldn't have married Mom if he knew.

We beg Mom not to marry him, and she tells us that he makes her happy and that we are ungrateful and just want her all to ourselves. She tells us that we are trying to ruin her life again and says that she'll never be happy without Ron. They go to City Hall and go through with the marriage.

Not much changes until Ron gets into a barroom brawl a couple months later. He basically gets the shit beat out of him for mouthing off to some guy. Ron ends up pulling out a gun, which we didn't even know he had, and shoots the guy that beat him up. He doesn't kill him, but the guy has to have major surgery and is in the hospital for more than three weeks. Ron and Mom have to take out huge loans to pay the guy's medical bills and to pay for Ron's lawyer. He ends up doing almost two years in jail over it, and when we hear that he's going away, Morgan and I are ecstatic!

And something even more incredible happens. Mom is mad at Ron for the first time ever. After he's been gone for about six months, she even talks about divorcing him before he gets out of jail. For a few months, we get our mom back. She's happy and fun. We eat dinner together and play board games at the kitchen table. On Saturday nights we make popcorn and watch movies together. Sometimes Morgan's there and sometimes she's not, and I really love the times that it's just me and Mom. We are broke, but we don't care—there is peace and harmony in our house for the first time ever.

Then it all changes. One day Mom accepts a collect call from Ron, and after that she starts going to visit him in jail. Pretty soon she's back to being his biggest fan. She tells me and Morgan that Ron was just defending himself; he shouldn't have gone to jail, and she can't wait until he's released and comes home. We are devastated but know that there's no changing her mind.

After Ron comes home, there is a small change. Being in jail really scared him, so he cuts back on his drinking. He's still a moody asshole to me, but at least he's a little bit nicer to Mom. Morgan moves out of the house right before Ron comes back. She's nineteen now, and she moves in with her boyfriend Dean.

Dean's a complete jerk and treats Morgan like crap, and I hate him from the first day I meet him. Morgan tells me that if I can't accept Dean, then she won't talk to me anymore. Gee, that sounds familiar. She ends up marrying him the following year, and I try to bite my tongue and put up with him to keep my relationship with my sister. My mom loves Dean, of course. Mom and Ron hang out with Morgan and Dean all the time, and they are quite the dysfunctional foursome. Mom and Morgan go on and on to each other about how happy they are and what great guys they are married to. Ron has mellowed out now that he's getting older, but he can still be a prick, but Dean is just a complete asshole to Morgan all the time.

***

A year before I meet Noah, I fly home for a visit and they decide to have a "family" barbeque at Dean and Morgan's house. It's just me, Mom, Dean, Morgan, and Ron at the barbeque. Jessica lives in Chicago and rarely comes home, so that's pretty much it for family.

Everything is going okay until Dean starts yelling at Morgan because she didn't buy him the right beer. She apologizes profusely and says she'll run right out to the grocery store and get him what he wants. He continues to yell at her, and I can't keep silent when he says, "Get your fat ass to the store and get my beer." Then he turns to Ron and says, "She's such a stupid bitch."

I stand up and warn him, "Don't you ever talk to her that way again, or I swear—"

He interrupts me and says, "Or what, huh? What are you going to do about it?"

Morgan and Mom are glaring at me, so I just say, "Why don't you get off of your useless ass and get your own damn beer?"

He is really in a rage now and tells Morgan, "Get that bitch out of here or I'm leaving."

Morgan is furious with me and tells me that I have no right to talk to her husband like that and to get out of her house. I go back to the hotel and decide to leave right then and there instead of the next night. I call the airline, and the soonest they can fly me out is five the next morning. I book it.

I fall asleep and wake up to my phone ringing at a little after nine that night. It's Mom. She lays into me about everything she can think of—I'm jealous of her and Morgan, I'm a loser, I got divorced twice because I don't know how to please a man, I need to apologize to Dean and Morgan, and on and on and on. I'm pretty much just letting her rant.

When she finally shuts up, I say, "Are you done now?"

"You know what I think the problem is? You don't like men. I think you're a lesbian." I can't believe she said that.

"Yep, Mom," I reply calmly, "You figured me out. I don't think we have anything else to say to each other." I hang up, and that's pretty much the last time I really talk to my mother. Morgan and I will eventually be on speaking terms again but, even so, I'll rarely hear from her.

# CHAPTER 23
# 2023

Our wine glasses are empty, so Jordan refills them for the last time because now the bottle is empty. We are warm and giggly from the wine, and we are both becoming flirtatious with each other.

We're sitting close on his couch, and I've touched his arm more times than I can count. He keeps brushing my hair off my face and letting his fingers trail down my neck when he does it, which gives me chills. I've taken off my sandals so I can stretch out my legs on his big, comfortable couch.

"How about a foot rub?" he offers.

I hesitate. I didn't expect that.

"Um…," he says, "I'm sorry, does that make you uncomfortable?"

"No," I quickly answer. "Um, sure, go ahead, I guess."

He asks again if I'm sure and I tell him yes. I feel that familiar electricity run through me as soon as he touches my foot. He starts gently massaging and says, "I can stop at any time, you just say the word. I don't want you to feel uncomfortable."

It feels incredible, and I relax immediately. I sigh and tell him it feels great. He spends at least ten minutes on my right foot and repeats the process with my left one. When he's done

I'm super relaxed. I have my head leaned back on the couch, and my eyes are closed. When I open my eyes, I see a big smile on his face.

"I'm glad you liked it. You deserve to be taken care of," he says.

"Well, let's see. You invited me to your house, cooked me dinner, took care of all the dishes, and gave me a foot massage. I think you have gone above and beyond tonight." I smile mischievously. "Now, how 'bout I return the favor?"

"Kate, you really don't have to do that. I didn't do it to get anything in return." I tell him that I'm positive that's not why he did it and that it would make me happy to do something for him. He finally agrees and takes his tennis shoes off.

"Socks off too, please," I say.

He smiles. "Okay, but I'm warning you, I'm ticklish."

"Got it. And I'll keep that in mind. Now give me your feet." He stretches both legs across me and I start massaging. He looks like he's in heaven and sighs contentedly.

"Oh my goodness, that's incredible. Do you have any idea how long it's been since I've had someone rub my feet? I forgot how good it feels." I take my time, and when I'm done I think he might actually be asleep. But he opens his eyes and says, "Thank you, Kate. That was fantastic."

And the next thing I know, we're hugging. I feel his warm breath as he's nuzzling my ear. I'm sure he can hear my heart beating because I can feel it thundering in my chest. I feel like it's suddenly become twenty-five degrees warmer in the house, and my ability to stay clearheaded is disappearing fast.

I finally manage to say, "Jordan, I think we'd better stop or I'm going to end up doing something I shouldn't."

"I was just going to say the same thing, but it's so hard to let you go."

We finally stop hugging and I look at the clock. It's after nine and, as difficult as it is, I say, "I should get going. And, um, I feel like I shouldn't drive because I only planned on one glass of wine, and that didn't happen." I laugh and he does too.

"Yeah," he says. "I guess we killed the bottle, didn't we? I shouldn't drive either. You could spend the night." He's smiling from ear to ear.

"You are really bad, aren't you? Tempting, but I should get an Uber, and then I can just Uber back and get my car in the morning if that's alright."

"Sure, but I'll come pick you up in the morning and bring you back here to get your car."

I hesitate again. Not the best idea to have him pick me up at my front door. "Actually, there's a little doughnut shop about three blocks from my place. I'll walk and meet you there in the morning."

"Yeah, sure," he agrees. "That's what we should do." Before I can pull my phone out, he's on his phone ordering my ride. It's going to arrive in about ten minutes, so I put my sandals on and tell him what a great night it's been. He says that he has had the best time too and then adds, "The next time we'll just plan ahead so driving isn't an issue."

I'm so happy he said that because that means we will be doing this again. My ride has arrived, so I give him one last long hug and we decide he will come pick me up at nine the next morning.

I get in the car and check my phone. Noah hasn't called, but I have three texts from Liz. She wants us to have retail therapy and lunch tomorrow afternoon. As she put it, her husband is being a "butthole" and she needs a girls' day. I smile because I love her choice of words. I send her a message and say sorry for my delayed response and that I would love some retail therapy too. I tell her that I have to do a couple things in the morning but how about one o'clock? She responds right away and says that sounds great and she'll pick me up then.

When I get home, I take Max out and get ready for bed. I debate calling Noah to tell him goodnight, but then I remember the time difference and decide that I'd better not since he's probably sleeping. Then I play every detail of the past three hours over and over in my mind and drift off to sleep.

\*\*\*

I'm up at six thirty the next morning. Noah calls at seven thirty and apologizes for not calling me last night. He says that he had a really long day and didn't even eat dinner until after ten. And by the time he got back to his room, he knew I would be asleep and didn't want to call and wake me up. I tell him no worries and that I figured that's what had happened.

I'm not prepared for him to ask, "So what did you do yesterday?"

"Um, you know, the usual. I took Max on a couple of long walks—"

"Aww, Max," he interrupts. "How is my baby? Does he miss me?"

I should be annoyed that he cut me off, but I'm glad that I don't have to talk about yesterday anymore. "Yeah, he misses you, of course. But he's been good." I suddenly realize that it's Sunday and I'll probably have to pick Noah up at the airport later.

Before I can ask he says, "Oh, my flight home doesn't get in until 7:10, which is later than usual, but can you pick me up?" I tell him of course I can and that I'll see him then.

After we hang up, I walk Max, shower, put on my makeup, and dry my hair. I head out the door at eight thirty to walk to the doughnut shop. The shop has muffins and bagels too, and sometimes I get their gluten-free blueberry muffins. They are delicious, and I decide to get a couple to take with me to Jordan's this morning. Just before nine, Jordan arrives and I get in his car.

"Good morning, beautiful. What do you have there?" I tell him that I have muffins and he says, "Perfect. Because I have a pot of coffee ready to go at home."

When we get to his house, he pours the coffee and puts the muffins on a plate. We sit down at the table, and he says, "I had the best time with you last night, Kate. But I was thinking…"

My heart sinks. Again, I'm thinking, is he going to put an end to this? Whatever this is.

He continues, "I hope that you aren't having doubts about us spending more time together." I'm surprised by what he's just said and ask him why he would think that.

"Well," he says, "I feel great about last night, and I know we really didn't do anything, but I went to bed worried that maybe I pushed it a little too far with the foot massage and all the—all the…body contact we had."

He's blushing now, and so am I. I try to think about how I want to respond without sounding like a babbling idiot, which seems to happen a lot when I'm with him. I take a deep breath. "Jordan, I initiated just as much as you did. I don't feel bad about anything we did last night either. And to be honest, I had a hard time not doing more. If anything is bothering me, it's the fact that I do want to do more."

I pause to take in his reaction and I'm relieved that he's still blushing and now has a big smile on his face. I continue, "It makes me happy to think that we will continue to spend more time together."

He wipes his hand across his forehead. "Phew. I'm so glad to hear you say that. And on the subject of spending more time together, how about next weekend we go to a movie on Friday night and then to the hot air balloon festival on Saturday evening? It's about an hour and a half drive from here. I don't know if you've ever been, but they light up all the balloons at sunset and it's really beautiful."

I give him an enthusiastic yes! Liz and I went the first year I moved out here and it was a lot of fun, so I'm excited to go again. I tell him that sounds like a perfect weekend to me. We both relax and enjoy our muffins and coffee. We sit and talk for two more hours and have three cups of coffee.

At around eleven thirty, I tell him that I should get going because I'm going to have girl time with Liz and she's picking me up at one.

"That's great. I hope you enjoy it and have a great afternoon. I'll miss you until I see you again." He tells me that he's going to get caught up on some laundry and that he really needs to do some things for work too. I tell him I'll miss him too, we hug, and I go out to his garage and get in my car. We give each other a quick wave as I leave.

Now what I'm worried about is Liz seeing this written all over my face. No one knows me like she does.

When I get home, I take Max out again and get some things done for the next day; I make my lunch, wash my uniforms and put them in the dryer, prep coffee and set the timer for five thirty the next morning.

Liz is in my driveway a little before one, and when I get in her car, I immediately say, "Hi! Okay, let's hear it. Why is Mark a butthole?"

Her response is great, "Because he's a man. Really, that's all. He's a man and just a complete turd sometimes. Enough said."

We both laugh and then launch into a discussion of "Why do they always have to...?" We spend at least fifteen minutes man-bashing while we drive to the restaurant. Our conversations are often a little on the vulgar side and full of sarcasm, and by the time we park, we are practically in tears from making each other laugh so hard! I'm glad that we have this distraction because I don't want to have to talk about what I'm up to.

We sit down to have lunch, and Liz says, "I feel like I haven't seen you forever! What's going on? How's work?" I tell her that work is good and that everything is fine. "Fine?" she responds and looks like she doubts me.

I quickly say, "Oh yeah, Noah got a promotion, but it means he has to travel a lot more. But it's more money, and he's happy to be moving up in the company."

"Oh no, I know how much you hate the travel part of his job. How do you feel about it?"

I tell her that at first I was upset about it, but I want to support him, so I'm trying to stay positive. I tell her that hopefully the travel will settle down over the next year and the sacrifice will be worth it.

"Well, at least when he comes home it's probably kind of nice, huh? Almost like your dating again, right?"

I lie. "Oh yeah, it makes things fun when he is home."

She smiles and says, "I bet! And you know I love Noah. He's such a great guy. So I guess you're right, just try to be patient." I tell her I agree and I'm glad that we're being interrupted by the waiter, whose nametag says "T. J.", asking us if we're ready to order. We decide to share a spinach and mushroom flatbread and both order iced tea.

T. J. says, "You got it. And I have to ask, are you two sisters?"

Without hesitation Liz says, "Yep, in fact we're twins." We really do look a lot alike—same height, same long blonde hair, and when we get together, we often show up only to find that we're wearing matching outfits, so we're used to hearing the sister thing.

T. J. is getting a little flirty. "I thought so. You guys looks so much alike." He looks at us a little too long and then says he'll be right back with our drinks. As he's walking away, Liz looks back at him and says softly so only I can hear her, "Come back, sexy, and let's run away together." We start laughing again and spend the next five minutes discussing how we hope he has a brother for me and where we'd run off to.

We enjoy our lunch, and the flirty waiter brings us a slice of cheesecake to share. I tell him we didn't order that, but he winks and says, "It's on the house. Didn't you know? Today is national twin sister celebration day." Pretty dorky, but it is free cheesecake after all.

We thank him and after he has turned around and is walking away, Liz mouths "I love you" to him and, again, we laugh so hard we are almost crying. After we pull ourselves together, we pay the bill and leave T.J. a big tip.

After we leave the restaurant, we go and do some shopping at our favorite clothing store. We both buy a couple of new tops and model them for each other when we come out of the dressing room. We assure each other that we look "smoking hot," and Liz tells me that Noah will love those tops on me. I feel a little pang of guilt because I'm thinking to myself that they're not for Noah.

Liz drops me off at home around five thirty. I put the laundry away, walk Max, and leave to go pick up Noah. While I'm driving to the airport, I'm wondering how Noah is going to act when he sees me this time.

When he gets in the car, he's not quite as over the top as he was the last time he returned from his trip. But I can see that he looks exhausted. As we're pulling away from the curb, he says, "I can't wait to get home, play with Max, take a shower, and go to bed."

I sympathize with the fact that he's exhausted, and I offer to take Max out for his last walk of the night so that he can crash early. He says that would be great. I ask him if he wants anything for dinner, but he says that he ate a big lunch earlier and isn't very hungry. After we've been driving for about ten minutes, he asks me how my weekend was and what I did. I'm glad that I was with Liz today because I give him a detailed description of everything we did. By the time I'm done talking, he doesn't ask me anything else, so I don't have to account for the rest of my time.

By the time we get home, it's already after eight o'clock. Noah tells me he'll unpack his bag tomorrow, throws the ball with Max for about ten minutes, takes a shower, and heads off to bed. I tell him that I'll be in shortly. I take Max out and finish my nighttime routine to get ready for bed. I try to sneak in the bedroom as quietly as I can because Noah is already sound asleep. I set the alarm for five and climb into bed.

***

I'm getting ready to leave for work the next morning, and just as I'm walking out the door, Noah comes out of the bedroom.

"Since you have a day off, what are you going to do today?" I ask him.

"I'll probably just hang out with Max and relax. I'm still tired from the trip", he says.

I tell him to have a great day and that I've got to run. Then I give him a quick kiss and leave for work.

Mondays are usually really busy, and today is no exception. I have back-to-back clients, and Dr. Taylor is busy with his regular schedule plus several emergency calls that came in. Dental emergencies always seem to happen over the weekend. If you're going to break a tooth or develop sudden pain, count on it being on Sunday night!

It's after one thirty before we finally get a breather, and we're all in the break room grabbing a quick bite before we have to go back and finish the afternoon. Anna is talking to Dr. Taylor. I overhear her say, "Dr. B., I don't know how much longer I can do this. I'm a senior citizen, you know, and today's schedule is elder abuse."

Dr. Taylor just laughs and says, "Oh, come on, it's not so bad. I know how much you love it. I'll probably have to kick you out when it's time for you to retire."

Anna rolls her eyes and says, "Ha. You wish! I'll be running for the door the day I turn sixty-five!"

Dr. Taylor just says, "We'll see. And now I have to get back to work, and so do you." She just gives him an exaggerated sigh, and he's laughing as he goes out the door.

Anna is the only one who calls him Dr. B. and the only one with enough nerve to talk to him with all her sarcasm. She has been with him for a long time, and they have a lot of respect for each other. I laugh and tell her that I wish I had the nerve to say some of the things she says. She smiles.

"Oh, whatever, I'll probably get my walking papers at the end of the day." And she knows that there is nothing further from the truth. I'm always grateful that I have her as my co-worker and my friend—she makes work fun, if that's possible.

The afternoon is just as busy as the morning, and we all work past closing time.

It's almost six thirty when I get in the car to head home. I text Noah to let him know I'm on my way. When I walk in the door, he's sitting on the couch with Max sleeping in his lap. He's watching a movie, and the volume is turned up ridiculously loud. I ask him if he can please turn it down a little.

He looks annoyed but says, "Sorry. Um, I didn't know what you wanted for dinner, so I didn't start anything."

"Well, there's a package of ground turkey and a package of chicken in the fridge, so I figured you'd know that it's one of those two choices." He just shrugs and tells me that burgers sound good.

I look at him for a few seconds in disbelief and then say, "Can you please get the grill going? I'll make the burgers." He sighs, apologizes to Max for having to get up and goes outside.

I make the burgers while I'm still in my work uniform, and after I'm done I go and put on my comfy lounging clothes. I throw a salad together while he grills the burgers. As I cut up the vegetables, I'm feeling more and more irritated. Before I know it, I've completely shredded the Romaine instead of just chopping it. I know that Noah worked all weekend and today is technically his Saturday, but would it have killed him to start dinner, especially since I worked an hour over tonight? I don't care if he hangs out on the couch all day, but he knows that I hate to eat past six thirty anyway, and tonight it's going to be almost eight before we sit down.

I don't say anything about eating so late and try to change my attitude. After all, I tell myself, I've got a lot of nerve being irritated, being as I spent my weekend with another man while Noah was busting his butt working. Now I'm just mad at myself.

After dinner Noah offers to help clear the dishes, but I tell him to just relax while I clean up the kitchen and make the coffee for tomorrow. While I'm cleaning up, he says that he's going to take Max out for the last time this evening. We've barely spoken since I came home because Noah wanted to keep the television on while we ate so he could see the end of the movie he was watching, even though it was one he's seen at least a half a dozen times.

As he's walking out the door, I say, "Hey, do you want to have a little glass of wine with me and talk for a bit when you get back? I feel like with you traveling and me working on your days off, we've barely seen each other."

He responds with, "Um, nah, I'm really tired. I think when I get back I'd rather just go to bed."

"I understand," I say, even though I'm disappointed that watching the movie during dinner was obviously more important than talking to his wife. After the door shuts, I pour myself a glass of wine and sit down with a book. I'm distracted and mostly just wondering what Jordan is doing right now.

***

The rest of the week is the same old routine—work, dinner, walking Max at night, and repeat. Noah leaves again on Thursday afternoon for week two of his six-to-eight-weekend travel commitment. This time he is traveling to South Carolina, and again, he tells me that communication will be hit and miss due to his schedule and the time difference. I tell him that I totally understand and just text me when he gets a chance.

Normally I would be more concerned with us staying in touch, but I have my own reasons for not communicating now. That guilty feeling rears its head again and quickly push it out of my mind. It's Thursday, and aside from a quick "Hi, how's your day?" I haven't talked to Jordan since I left his house on Sunday. During my lunch break, I'm sitting in my car with the windows down and I decide to text him:

**Hi, handsome. How are you? I hope you've been having a good week. I've been thinking about you.**

I hit send, eat my yogurt, and enjoy the silence. I always park my car at the very end of the parking lot so I can have some uninterrupted quiet time, even if my lunch is only fifteen or twenty minutes long. My phone chimes and I read Jordan's reply:

**_Well hello, beautiful! I'm good but must admit that I'm counting the hours until I see you tomorrow. Are you good with meeting at the market again and heading to the movie theater from there? How about 6:00?_**

I tell him that sounds like a plan and that I'll see him tomorrow. I go back to work and finish the rest of my workday. I'm thrown for an unexpected loop at closing time. I've just shut the light off in my exam room when Anna comes around the corner and says, "Hey Kate, your husband's working out of town this weekend, right?"

"Um, yeah, why?"

"Well, that new café on Lincoln Street finally opened and Yvonne, Mindy, and I were talking about checking it out tomorrow night. You'll come with us, right?"

I'm struggling to think of an excuse, and Anna is looking at me, waiting for an answer. I finally manage to spit out, "Oh, I wish I'd known! I just made plans for tomorrow night when I was on my lunch break. Liz's husband is going bowling with his buddies, and she asked me to go see a movie with her." Okay, I reason with myself, it's only half a lie—I really am going to see a movie.

Anna seems to believe what I just said, even though I don't think I sounded convincing at all, and says, "Bummer. We'll have to plan ahead a little better next time. We'll miss you."

"Yeah, sorry, but definitely let me know how it is. If it's good, we'll go soon." We say goodnight, wish each other a good weekend, and head to our cars.

I feel terrible for lying to Anna, but I'm thinking there's no way I'm going to miss any time I get with Jordan. That guilty feeling is back and I don't like it.

When I get home I change my clothes and take Max out for a walk. I'm not very hungry, so I decide to just have some cheese and crackers for dinner. I pour myself a glass of wine out of the bottle I opened last night and sit down on the couch. After I eat, I turn the television on and lie down on the couch. I'm startled by the sound of my text alert going off on my phone. I fell asleep—my phone says it's 9:44. The text is from Noah:

*Hi. I know you are already sleeping, but I just wanted to message you before I went to bed. It was a really long day and I'm exhausted. I've got two meetings tomorrow morning and four clinics I have visit in the afternoon, so I'll probably be out of touch again tomorrow. Sorry. Enjoy your day off tomorrow. Love you.*

I feel bad. Really bad. I decide to call Noah. I'll just tell him that I was having trouble sleeping and I'm still up. I call, but it goes to voicemail. It's only been four minutes since he sent me that message. There's no way he could be asleep already, right? He probably put his phone on silent right after he texted me so he would be sure to get good, uninterrupted sleep. I usually don't leave a message, but tonight I decide to:

"Hi. I just got your text. I'm having trouble sleeping and so I'm still awake. Hope you sleep well and you have a good day tomorrow. Don't worry about not being able to text or call—I know you're very busy. Liz and I are going to a movie Saturday night so I'll get errands done tomorrow. Love you."

Now when Noah asks, I won't have to come up with an answer for what I did on Saturday night. I'm becoming accustomed to lying and I don't like it; it's definitely not who I am. I try not to think about it anymore and whistle for Max. I put him on the leash but just take him out in the front yard because it's late. When we come in, I make sure the house is locked up, Max curls up in his dog bed in the living room, and I head off to bed.

I really do have trouble sleeping, but I know that I deserve it for lying to people I love. Lying and cheating are things I've always said I wouldn't tolerate in a relationship, and now look at what I'm doing. I try to silence my thoughts, but I still can't sleep. The last time I look at the clock, it's almost two in the morning.

# CHAPTER 24
# 2016

Liz and her family have just moved to Nevada, and I'm miserable. Vincent and I broke up two years ago, and I really haven't dated much since then. It's a brutally cold winter, so when I'm not working, I spend all my time at home. I'm bored and start thinking about how much I hate the cold weather and contemplate moving, maybe to where Liz and her family relocated to. Every time she and I talk on the phone and I tell her it's twenty degrees where I am and she tells me that it's seventy degrees where she is, I ask myself why in the world I'm still here. My job is really the only thing keeping me in Iowa.

One Saturday night one of the girls at my office asks me if I want to join her and a few others and go out. At first I say no, but then I decide that a night out sounds pretty good. It's early December, but there are already more than six inches of snow on the ground, and on the night that we go out, it's a balmy twelve degrees. It's impossible to dress in anything other than something that resembles a snowsuit when it's this cold. I bundle up in jeans, a base layer top, a heavy sweater, boots, a hat, gloves and my heaviest coat and get an Uber to pick me up.

When I get to the bar, the girls, all of them seven to ten years younger than me, are already well into several rounds of drinks, based on the number of glasses on the table.

"Kate!" I hear someone yell. I turn to the voice, and it's my coworker Mary, who invited me. She's waving me over to the table a little too enthusiastically, probably because she's already had several shots.

I go over to the table, take off my huge coat, and they immediately order me a shot and tell me that I need to catch up. Despite their insistence I sip it slowly. Shots aren't my thing, and I would really rather have a glass of wine or a beer. But there is a good band playing and we all hit the dance floor. I must admit I'm having fun, but by eleven, I'm ready to go home.

"No, Kate," Mary says, "We're all going to another club down the street. Come with us!"

I tell her that I can't but to go and have a great time and that I'll see her at work on Monday. She tries a few more times to convince me, but I insist on going home and they leave. I decide that I should use the bathroom before I head home, and when I get back to the table, there's a guy sitting there. I assume he thinks the table is free because we all left, even though my coat is still on my chair. I lean over him to grab it.

"Excuse me, I just need to get my coat." We make brief eye contact as I'm grabbing my coat. He smiles at me.

"Leaving? Too bad, I was hoping I could get a dance with you." I had seen him looking at me earlier. He was sitting with a couple of other guys at the end of the bar, but I didn't pay much attention to him because he's not my typical type at all. He's very tall and thin. His hair is slicked back, and the clothes he's wearing haven't been in style for at least ten years. But he does have a nice smile.

"Thanks, but I need to get going," I say.

"Well, I might as well go too, since the most beautiful girl in the place is leaving." I'm thinking that was a cliché line but decide to just go with it.

"Well, I suppose one dance wouldn't kill me."

"It's my lucky day. I'm Colton, by the way. Let's go." There's a slow song playing, and we look like we are at an eighth-grade dance. I think he's trying to be a gentleman and there is at least two feet of space between us. As ridiculous as we look, I like that he's being respectful and I'm enjoying myself.

We end up staying for one more drink and three more dances, each time getting a little closer together. It's almost one in the morning when I tell him I really have to go. We exchange phone numbers and he walks me to the door.

We start dating after that. He's a nice guy and he has a good job. It's not long before we're spending every weekend together. After about three months of dating, he tells me that he's getting kicked out of his apartment because the guy who owns the building sold it and the new owner wants to tear it down and put up all new condos at three times the rent. He tells me about it one night after we'd been out having dinner, and I ask him where he's going to move to.

"Well, what if I moved in with you? I love you and I see a future with you. I know we didn't plan this, but I want to be with you. I want to be with you all the time."

I have some reservations, and he sees my hesitation.

"I understand if you don't want to," he says. "It is a little fast. You know, it would probably be better if I just find a place near work. But then I probably won't get to see you very much at all." He works about forty minutes from where we both currently live, and I don't like the thought of us only seeing each other on weekends, and sometimes not even that if the weather is bad and the roads are closed.

I should have seen that first red flag of manipulation, but I missed it completely. I tell him that I don't want us living far apart, and I'd be thrilled to have him move into my house with me.

By the following weekend, Colton and his best friend are in my driveway with a moving truck full of all his belongings. He's got a lot of stuff, and I'm trying to figure out where it's all going to go in my small house. By the time they're done unloading it all, every room is full, along with a good amount of space in the garage.

"I'm going to take Eric out for a beer to thank him for helping me," Colton tells me. "See you in a few hours."

I'm shocked. I can't believe he just moved in with me, and on the very first night, he's leaving and didn't even invite me to come along. Red flag number two.

That day is the beginning of me seeing the real Colton. My house is just a place for him to flop. He is either working, spending the weekend at Eric's house playing video games until late, or playing pool in a co-ed billiard league. We rarely go out at all anymore, and he's becoming critical of everything I do, say, and wear. Whenever I try to talk to him about it, he says that I'm nagging and that's why he doesn't want to be around me anymore.

When we are about five months into our relationship, I catch him on the phone with another woman. I come home from work early and he doesn't hear me come in. I hear him saying, "Yeah, I know. I miss you too. It's not going to be much longer…" As I come around the corner, he rushes out, "I have to go" and hangs up.

"Who was that? It was Diane wasn't it?" Diane is on his billiard league. I met her once when the league had a dinner get together and everybody brought their significant other. My instincts told me immediately that if she and Colton didn't have something going on at that time, they wanted to. They were smiling and giving each other little glances all night long. On the way home from the dinner, I accused him of having something going on with her and he became very angry. He told me that I was crazy, and if I kept it up I was going to drive him away, so I ended up apologizing profusely and agreed with him that I was acting completely crazy. Red flag number three.

He puts his phone down and says "Yes, it was Diane. She's upset because she's fighting with her boyfriend. We are just good friends and she misses my company. I was just assuring her it wouldn't be long until league night and that I miss her company too."

My gut feeling is that he's lying, but I say, "Okay, if you say so. But I still don't like her calling you and confiding in you. Doesn't she know that we are a couple and that's inappropriate?"

He sighs and grabs my shoulders. Then he looks me right in the eyes and says, "We are just friends. You are my girlfriend, and I love you. And if you don't stop all this, you are going to ruin our relationship."

As usual, I apologize and ask him to please forgive me.

He says he needs time to think and is going to spend the weekend at Eric's.

Our relationship limps along for another month, and his absences from home become more frequent. One night I come home from work and he tells me that we need to talk.

"This just isn't working out," he says. "I'm not happy, and you won't ever be able to make me happy. I'm leaving."

Immediately I know what's changed. "It's Diane, isn't it?"

He doesn't even try to deny it. "Yes, I love her, and I want to be with her."

Now I'm furious. "I knew it! All this time you tried to make me think I was crazy! You lying sack of shit!"

"It's going to take me a while to find a place, so I'll live here until then," he says. I'll just stay in the guest room."

I stare back in disbelief. "You've got to be kidding, right?! No way. Get out now! You can come get your shit later."

He tells me he has nowhere to go, and I tell him to go move in Diane since they are so in love! He actually tries to talk me into letting me stay, but I kick him out right then and there. I text him the next day and let him know that I will be out of the house all day the following Saturday. I tell him to come get his stuff and leave his keys on the kitchen table. He says he isn't sure if he can get everything out in one day, and I tell him he better try because anything he leaves behind is going to be put in a pile and set on fire. Not really, but I wanted every trace of him gone!

He manages to get everything that Saturday, and I never hear from him again. He and Diane break up just a couple of months later (shocking) and according to one of his friends, no one has seen him since.

After he's gone I decide I need a change. I call Liz and tell her that I'm going to move to Nevada. Actually, I should thank Colton for putting me through hell because moving to Nevada is the best decision I have ever made.

# CHAPTER 25
# 2023

It's 5:45, and I'm already waiting for Jordan in the parking lot of the market. I slept until after eight this morning and took a nap in the early afternoon because I barely slept at all last night. About ten minutes later, Jordan pulls in next to me. I can't believe how happy I am to see him. I know that it's only been a few days, but I feel like I haven't seen him in months. I get in his car, and I'm greeted warmly.

"Hi! I couldn't wait to see you today," he gushes.

I tell him that I feel the same way. We give each other a quick hug and leave for the thirty-minute drive to the theater. Conversation flows easily between us on the drive, and I'm relieved. I can relax and focus and enjoying myself. We get to the theater, and I tell him it's his turn to pick the movie tonight.

"Hmm, well we did action last time, so let's do romance tonight."

"Are you sure?" I prompt. "You don't have to just because you think that's what I want to see."

He looks serious and says, "Kate, first of all, that's not why I picked it. But if I was choosing it to make you happy, then there's nothing wrong with that. You should be okay with someone doing things for you once in a while. And second of all, I really do want to see it. I like all kinds of movies, and based on the previews, it looks like it's a good one."

"You're right, and I really do want to see this one too." We decide to get popcorn and take our seats. The movie is really good—it's got some funny parts but a couple of sad parts too. I tear up a couple of times, and Jordan squeezes my hand when I do.

After the movie he asks if I want to get coffee. I tell him I'd love to but I did not sleep well at all last night so caffeine probably isn't the best idea.

"Okay, sure," he says. "How about ice cream then?"

"That sounds wonderful." I realize that aside from the movie popcorn, all I had to eat today was scrambled eggs and toast this morning and some yogurt and fruit for lunch. We get our ice cream and decide to eat it in the car. It's a beautiful night, and we are parked in an empty parking lot next door to the ice cream shop with the car windows down, enjoying the warm evening air.

Halfway through his cone, Jordan turns to me and says, "There were a couple parts of the movie that were really sad, huh? I got a little choked up."

"Oh yeah, some of it was hard for me to watch."

He nods. "I'd like to know more about you, Kate. I know you told me a little bit about Noah and a little about your relationships before him, but what was your childhood like?"

I laugh and say, "As far as my childhood goes, there's not enough time to go into that. And past relationships? I'll tell you more about them, but I just don't want to get into too much detail. There's a lot that I'd rather not think about." I look down sheepishly.

"Hey, I don't mean to push you, and you don't have to feel pressured to tell me anything."

I take a deep breath and say, "No, Jordan, I want you to know about me. It's just that some of it is really embarrassing. I mean when I look back on a lot of things, it's humiliating that I allowed some guys to treat me the way they did."

He's finished his ice cream by now. He reaches over, takes my hand, and rubs my shoulder, so I start talking. I tell him a little bit more about Greg, Vincent, and Colton, but I don't want to talk about the abusive relationship I had with Alex, so I don't, and he doesn't push.

When I'm done talking, he says, "Wow, Kate. You've had a rough time with relationships. I'm so sorry that you had to go through that, and I'm so proud of you for what you were able to overcome."

"Thank you for saying that. I really appreciate it. But I have to take partial blame because sometimes I allowed myself to be treated poorly, and I didn't value myself enough to get out sooner. Now, will you tell me a little bit about your childhood?"

He leans back and says, "Sure, um, my childhood was pretty normal, I guess. I'm an only child. My parents didn't think they could have children, and I wasn't born until my mom was thirty-eight and my dad was forty-one." He pauses for a moment before continuing.

"They were great parents, and it was tough to lose my dad when I was seventeen. He got colon cancer, diagnosed late, and he died within weeks of his diagnosis. After that my mom just sort of shut down. She gave up on life and pretty much became a recluse. She was always this beautiful, vibrant lady, and all of a sudden, she just quit taking care of herself."

Now it's my turn to grab his hand and squeeze. "By the time I was twenty-two, I had to put her in an assisted living facility because I couldn't trust her to eat or take care of the house. Even though she was only sixty, she couldn't function by herself anymore."

"Oh, Jordan, that's really tough. Are you still close with her? Do you go and visit her?"

His eyes fill with tears and he says, "I used to. When she was in assisted living, I went to see her at least three times a week. But about a year ago, she was diagnosed with Alzheimer's. I had to move her to a nursing home, and she doesn't know me anymore." His voice breaks then. "I used to go visit a few times a week, but now my being there gets her very agitated and upset, so I only go about once a month. When I see her now, it's not my mom. It's like going to see a stranger, you know? When I walk in, I always say, 'Hi mom, it's me, Jordan. You look pretty today,' and she always smiles and seems calm for a few minutes, but then she gets very upset and starts screaming and crying, so I leave. The nurses tell me that she calms down after I'm gone, so I just try to stay away now."

A tear rolls down his cheek, and I'm tearing up too. I take my hand and wipe the tear off his face. He shakes his head and says, "Geez, sorry. That was way more information than you needed and it was depressing."

"Hey, don't ever apologize for talking about your parents. I'm so happy you felt comfortable enough with me to share that, and I'm just so sorry that has happened to your mom. I guess if she was a good mom and you guys had a good relationship, then those are the memories that you need to hold onto now."

Jordan smiles at me. "Yeah, you're right. I have so many good memories of her. She was a great mom."

We've both finished our ice cream now and it's almost ten thirty, so we decide we'd better head back to my car. When we get to the parking lot, I tell him what a wonderful night I had and thank him for everything.

"Tomorrow is going to be really fun. No heavy conversations, I promise. Let's just have a good time." I tell him that sounds great and that I'm really looking forward to it. I suggest meeting in the parking lot of the restaurant that Liz and I had lunch at last weekend, and we decide to leave at three thirty due to the hour-and-a-half drive it will take to get to the balloon festival.

He gets out and opens the car door for me. We give each other a long hug, and he tells me that I better sleep well tonight. I promise him that I will. As always, he waits until he sees me pull out of the lot before he starts to drive away. I glance at my phone at the first red light I come to and see that Noah sent me a short text just before nine thirty:

*Hey, Kate. I know that you're asleep by now. Just wanted to let you know that I just got back to my room. I'm exhausted and going to bed. I'll try to text or call you sometime during the day tomorrow if I get a break. Kiss Max for me. Love you.*

Again, it was almost twelve thirty in the morning where he is when he texted me, and I keep thinking that his schedule must be insane. And I know how he is—he probably gets done with dinner and is back in his room before eleven but stays up and goes through his email and researches the clinics/hospitals he will be visiting the next day. He likes to be prepared, and that's more important to him than sleep.

By the time I get home, I'm exhausted. Max gets another front-yard-only walk. Then I fill his food and water bowls and get myself ready for bed. I fall asleep almost immediately and don't wake up until after eight the next morning.

After I get up, I take Max to the dog park and we play for over an hour. Even though Noah's over-the-top attachment to him gets on my nerves, I do like the dog and feel like I've been neglecting him. We throw the Frisbee and tennis ball until we're both worn out.

When we get home, he eats, drinks, and then goes to his doggy bed, where he sleeps for most of the day. I get busy cleaning the kitchen, doing laundry, and vacuuming.

It's about four o'clock where Noah is, so I decide to give him a call in the hope that I'll catch him before he goes to dinner. To my surprise he answers.

I ask him how his day is going, and he says, "I'm exhausted and I've got one more clinic to visit. Then I'm going to have dinner and go to bed right after that."

"I'm sorry you are having to work so hard. Try to get to bed early and get some good rest," I respond. Then he asks me how Max is doing. I tell him we went to the dog park this morning and he's happy to hear that.

He lets out an exhausted sigh and says, "Well, I've got to go."

I'm grateful that he didn't ask me anything about going to the movies with Liz. We say "love you" to each other and hang up.

I shower and put my makeup on. I've got that giddy, butterflies in my stomach feeling as I finish up with a swipe of shimmery pink lip gloss. And I find myself wondering if or when Jordan might kiss me. I try to push those thoughts out of my head and, instead, turn my attention to what I should wear tonight. It's another warm night, and it's a little windy because there is a storm front moving in that's supposed to bring rain to the area, so I choose a pair of denim capris, one of the new tops I bought when Liz and I went shopping, and slip-on tennis shoes. I decide on a ponytail because I don't want to have to deal with my long hair blowing in my face all night. I wake Max up for a quick trip outside and then head out to meet Jordan.

# CHAPTER 26
# 2023

I pull into the parking lot of the restaurant five minutes late, and Jordan is already there waiting for me. As soon as I park, he's out of his car to open the door for me. I immediately apologize for being late.

"Look at you," he replies. "You are well worth the wait. You look so pretty." I tell him thank you and that he looks great too. And he really does.

We talk effortlessly on the ninety-minute drive and arrive at the festival a little past five. We head up to the gate, and despite my protests, Jordan pays for both of us to get in. Admission includes one food and drink ticket, so we head over to get a burger and a beer. There are at least fifty balloons, and we try to see all of them while we walk around eating our burgers. By the time we've walked all over, it's getting close to dusk and the balloons are starting to be lit. When it's completely dark, it's beautiful to see the glow from all the balloons.

We are standing and admiring a bright blue balloon that looks even more amazing when it's glowing when from behind me I hear, "Kate?" My blood immediately runs cold. I don't recognize the voice, but obviously it's someone who knows me.

I turn, and I'm confused at first because I don't recognize the guy who's talking to me. He sees the confusion on my face and says, "It's me. Jeff Baldwin. You do my cleanings every six months." Now I remember.

"Oh, sorry, Jeff. I didn't recognize you at first. How are you?"

"I'm good. I'll be coming to see you in about three weeks." Then he looks at Jordan like he's expecting an introduction, but I just say, "That's great. I look forward to seeing you then."

He looks at Jordan one more time and then back at me before pointing toward his left, saying, "Yeah, my wife and kids are wandering around somewhere over there, so I'd better go. Good to see you."

I tell him goodbye and to enjoy his evening. Then I turn back to Jordan and say, "I'm so sorry. I wasn't prepared for that. I really didn't think about seeing anyone I know this far from home."

"I honestly hadn't thought about that either, but you handled it really well," he says.

We walk around a little longer, but now I'm anxious and looking around to make sure I don't see anyone else that I know, and I'm pretty sure that Jordan is doing the same thing. I don't think he had considered how he would respond if he ran into someone he knew either. After about ten minutes, he says, "What do you think? Ready to go?" I nod in agreement and only relax when we're both back in his car.

After we've been driving for about thirty minutes, we pass a little bar out in the middle of nowhere and we decide to stop for a drink. We are the only two people in the place, and it feels good to know we can just relax and enjoy our time together. After we finish our beer, we sit and talk for about an hour and then head for home.

On the rest of the ride home, Jordan either has his hand on my knee or he's lightly running his fingers up and down my thigh. I'm aching for more and marveling at how he seems to know exactly how to touch me. I return the favor by lightly stroking his ear and his neck. He sighs, and after about a minute he says, "If you keep that up, I'm going to have to pull over."

Reluctantly, I say, "Okay, you're right, maybe we'd better stop torturing each other."

We both laugh. "Who knew that torture could feel so good?" Jordan says.

We are both smiling, enjoying the music on the radio, and not saying anything for the last ten minutes of the ride. I imagine he's got some of the same thoughts going through his head that are going through mine. When we get to parking lot, he pulls up next to my car, puts the windows down, and turns the engine off. After he unbuckles his seat belt, he turns, looks me in the eyes, and says, "How do I say this? I hope I don't offend you, but I'm just going to say it. Here goes. You turn me on more than you can even imagine, and I want you, Kate."

I didn't expect him to say anything like that, and before I can stop it, I start to giggle nervously. I quickly pull myself together. "Wow. Well, I'm not offended. And I have to tell you that I lose all my senses when you touch me, Jordan, and you definitely get my heart racing." He's giving me that big smile that I love so much.

"Well, just so you know. That's just the beginning, I would love to spend hours touching you and making you feel good."

I can feel my cheeks turning bright red. I drop my head, and all I can manage to whisper is, "Same."

After what feels like eternity, he says, "Well, I think we've established that we are enormously attracted to each other." I nod in agreement. He changes the subject and says, "That was pretty crazy running into someone you knew tonight, huh?"

"I really don't know him, he's just a patient of mine, but it does make me think that it's dangerous for us to be seen in public. I mean, going to the movie theater is perfect because it's far away and we're sitting in the dark, but going forward maybe we should be a little more careful."

I'm worried that he's going to be upset by what I just said, but instead he says, "Well, more steaks and foot massages at my place it is then." I nod enthusiastically in agreement and say that, unfortunately, it's getting late and we better call it a night. He walks me to my car.

"What are you doing tomorrow, beautiful?"

"Not much because I did all of my errands on Friday," I reply.

"Well, it's supposed to be rainy and cool tomorrow. How would you like to come to my place in the afternoon? We could close the blinds, turn on the fireplace, and watch a movie if you want." I tell him that sounds perfect on a rainy day and ask what time.

"How about one? I'll leave the garage open for you." I tell him I'll see him then, we give each other one more hug, and I get in my car and drive home.

Once I'm in bed, I can't stop thinking about how he touched me earlier tonight, and then I'm picturing his hands all over me...

# CHAPTER 27
# 2023

I wake up just before six, which is more my usual time, and after I brush my teeth and take Max out, I do my most butt-kicking circuit workout. After I shower and have a little breakfast, I check my phone and see that Noah texted me at three thirty this morning:

*Good morning. It's 6:30 here. I'm having breakfast at the hotel and then I have to go visit two more clinics today. My flight home got changed and now I'm not getting in until 8:40, which I'm not happy about. It might get delayed even more, based on the weather report I'm looking at—is it raining there yet? Anyway, I'll take an Uber home, so don't worry about having to come and get me. If my flight gets delayed any further, I'll let you know. Otherwise, I should be home a little before 10 tonight. Hope you have a good day.*

I feel bad for him. He just wants to get home, and now who knows how late it might be. It's supposed to get stormy here later today, so it could cause more problems for him. My second selfish thought is that I won't have to rush home from Jordan's. I send Noah a response:

*Good morning. So sorry your flight got changed. It's not raining here yet, but it's cloudy and windy and the rain is supposed to start sometime in the afternoon. I hope you don't have any more delays. See you soon.*

I do a little meal prep for the week and make sure everything is ready to go for the workweek ahead. After I'm done with all of that, I put on my makeup, curl my hair, and get dressed. I decide that if we are going to just be sitting on the couch watching a movie, I want to be super comfortable. I put on a pair of cozy jogger sweatpants, a T-shirt, and flip flops. I also grab a hoodie to take with me because the temperature is supposed to drop when the rain moves in.

Just as I'm pulling into Jordan's driveway, the rain starts. He greets me with a big smile and hug and tells me he's so happy I'm there. "What can I get you?"

"Nothing right now, thanks."

"Okay, but later I have snacks and a glass of wine for us."

"That sounds perfect," I say.

"Now don't make fun of me, but I actually own a ton of movies." He takes me to his office and opens a huge file cabinet drawer full of movies. "So why don't you look through them and pick something?" He has them all lined up in alphabetical order, and I'm seriously impressed that he took the time to do that. He literally has something from every genre, and I take my time deciding.

"Well, we've done action and romance, so how about something a little scary?" I suggest.

"On a stormy day that sounds perfect." He asks me to please have a seat on the couch. Then he closes all the blinds, dims the lights very low, and lights a couple of candles.

"Spooky!" I tell him.

"Well, if you get scared, you can just scoot closer to me."

"That just might happen," I smirk, then we start the movie. Even though I've seen it before and I'm not the least bit scared, I sit pretty close to him and we hold hands.

When the movie is over, we sit at the kitchen island, nibble on meatballs, cheese, and bread, and have a glass of Merlot. He asks if I want more wine, but I say that I don't have the option of not driving later so I'm limited to one glass.

"Do you mind if I have another?" he asks.

"Of course not. Please, enjoy yourself. If I didn't have to drive, I'd join you."

He refills his glass while I go to use the bathroom. I want to brush my teeth, and I'm glad I keep a little toothbrush and floss in my purse. When I come out, Jordan is waiting for me on the couch. He is minty fresh too, and it makes me smile that we both went and did the same thing. He offers to put on something else to watch.

"Sure, that's fine." I say.

He does a quick search and puts on a romantic comedy from the '80s. It's a movie I know well and really like. He takes a sip of his wine and asks me if I'm comfortable. I tell him that I'm very comfortable, and right after that we hear thunder off in the distance. The rain is getting louder and louder, and the wind is picking up.

"Mind if I turn a local station on for a bit?" I tell him that's fine, and we find a station that's talking about the weather. They say that the rain should stop by around seven thirty but to be prepared for a lot of lightning and heavy downpours.

Jordan smiles and says, "Well, I guess you'd better stay until at least seven thirty. I mean, just for safety reasons. You don't want to drive in that, do you?"

I smile and say, "No, absolutely not. I'd better stay awhile then." It's only a little before six, and I'm happy that we get more time, but then I start thinking about Noah getting delayed and having to fly during bad weather. That familiar guilty feeling returns, and I try to push it away.

Jordan turns the volume way down so we can barely hear the TV and drinks the last sip of his wine. He sets his glass down and says, "Come closer. I want to put my arm around you, if that's alright with you." I scoot in under his arm. He wraps his arms around me, and I lean into him.

141

He's gently stroking my arm and then moves my hair off my neck. I inhale sharply when I feel his lips gently graze my cheek and move down my neck. He spends a good amount of time planting soft, slow kisses up and down the side of my neck over and over again. My arms have exploded with goosebumps and I feel like I'm melting into him. He notices my goosebumps, smiles, and says, "I take it you like your neck kissed, Kate."

"Well, I didn't know that before now, but I guess I do. Do you like your neck kissed?"

He hesitates and says, "Yeah, I sure do. But…um, it almost feels too good, like I can hardly stand it. It gets me going like crazy."

I'm surprised by what he just said, and he's blushing. I respond, "Hmm, interesting. I'd like to test it for myself, if that's all right with you."

"I'd really like that, but if it gets too intense I might have to ask you to stop, okay?"

I nod in agreement and sit up on my knees. "Just lean back and enjoy," I say. Then I run my fingertips from his wrists all the way up his arms and back down again. I'm pleased to see that his arms are now covered in goosebumps too. He sighs in appreciation, and I continue by throwing my leg around him, basically straddling him, so I can have access to both sides of his neck. His eyes open in shock because he wasn't expecting that, then he just smiles and closes his eyes again.

I lean forward and brush my lips across his left ear and kiss my way all the way down and back up the side of his neck in the same way he just did to me. He's breathing heavily, and I can literally hear his heartbeat. I do this a few more times and make my way over to his right ear. I kiss up and down the right side of his neck a couple of times and then repeat the whole process.

After a couple of minutes, he opens his eyes and says, "Kate, you are killing me. You have to stop." I hesitate but agree that it's getting really hot in here and climb off of his lap.

He goes to the fridge and gets us both a bottle of water and wipes his brow with the bottle before he opens it. He chugs down almost the entire bottle and then just smiles and shakes his head at me.

"What?" I ask.

"You are amazing, you know that? I can't get enough of you, and the only reason I made you stop is because I couldn't trust myself if you did that for much longer. You know exactly how to touch me, and I just want more and more of you."

He just said the same thing I was thinking, so I just smile at him and say, "Same."

We sit close and talk while we listen to the storm outside become quieter and quieter until the rain stops altogether. I tell him that, unfortunately, I should get going. We are both sad and it's getting harder and harder for us to be away from each other.

He says, "So, what should we do next weekend?"

I think for a second and then say, "Well, how about this? I come over on Saturday night, but I cook for you this time. I have a good recipe for pasta with shrimp and scallops."

"That sounds like a great idea." I tell him the dish is a little labor intensive, so if I could come at around three and start getting it ready that would be great. He says the earlier the better.

I say, "My friends at work are starting to get suspicious about what I'm up to every weekend, so I think I'm going to ask them to go to dinner on Friday night."

He says that's a good idea and that he will probably get together with one of his friends on Friday night too. I thank him for an informative and wonderful evening and go in for a hug.

"Informative?" he asks.

"Yeah, I'm learning the road map of where to touch you and how to make you squirm. You know, that torture we talked about last night."

We both laugh, and he says, "Oh yes, it was very informative for me too, and you just get ready because I think I might feel like torturing you *a lot* next Saturday."

I feel myself shiver with excitement and tell him I'm already looking forward to it. I get in my car, we wave goodbye to each other, and I head for home. The storm has passed and it's just drizzling rain now.

When I get home, it's a little past seven thirty. I don't have any more messages from Noah, so I know that his flight didn't get delayed further. I take Max out for a walk, wash my face, and curl up on the couch with a book. I keep having to re-read the same thing over and over because all I can think about is how Jordan was touching me earlier and how I was touching him. And I keep replaying the last thing he said to me: "You just get ready because I think I might feel like torturing you *a lot* next Saturday." He really emphasized *a lot*, and I can't stop thinking about what he might do to me.

I finally slam the book shut and turn on the television. I lie down on the couch, and the next thing I know, I hear the key in the door. Noah is home. I look at the clock, and it's just past ten. He's surprised to see me and says, "You weren't waiting up for me, were you?"

I feel like an asshole because I wasn't, but I lie and say, "I was trying to, but I guess I fell asleep." He drops his bag off in his office, and Max is all over him. After he's done petting and hugging Max, he comes over and gives me a hug. I ask him if he's hungry, and he says he is.

"Why don't you go ahead and get in the shower, and I'll make you a sandwich?" He tells me that sounds good, and I put together a turkey and Swiss cheese sandwich for him.

After he gets out of the shower, he tells me that I don't have to stay up with him. "I'm off tomorrow, but you have to work so feel free to go on to bed if you want." I tell him that I worked out today and won't have to tomorrow, so I can sleep in a little later. I sit at the kitchen island with him while he eats his sandwich and tells me all about his trip.

"Oh," he says, "Because I put in so many hours this weekend and got in so late tonight, they're giving me Wednesday off too."

"That's great," I say and hope that my face didn't show that for a moment I was afraid he was going to say they were giving him next weekend off. I ask him where he's traveling to next weekend, and he tells me South Carolina again. His company has acquired two more practices there. He has to go and visit the new practices in person, plus continue some additional work with the four accounts they already have.

"It's a bummer that you have to travel that far again," I say.

"It will all be worth it in the end, Kate. Just a few more weekends and then I'll be back to my regular once or twice a month travel to Sacramento. I might have to go back out East here and there, but at least the every-weekend travel will be over."

I give him my best fake smile and say that I can't wait, but I'm hurting inside over the fact that, at some point, whatever Jordan and I have is going to have to end. I tell him I'd better get some sleep, and he says he's going to check his email and will be in shortly. I give him a quick kiss and head off to bed.

# CHAPTER 28
# 2023

Anna rushes up to me first thing when I get to the office on Monday morning, "Kate! You really should have come with us Friday night. That new restaurant is amazing. The food was so good, and they make killer margaritas!"

And before I can answer, Anna adds, in typical Anna style, "And our waiter was hot! But he was wearing some really tight pants. I mean, he might as well have been naked from the waist down, know what I mean?" I'm laughing pretty hard and now she's laughing too and says, "I'm just sayin'."

"Well, would you want to go back this Friday?," I ask.

Anna emphatically answers, "Uh, yeah!" and then says she will ask Yvonne and Mindy if they can come too. I tell her that sounds great, and while we're getting our rooms ready for our first patients of the day she's telling me all about the food they ordered and what she wants to try when we go on Friday.

The day is busy, as usual, and I don't get my lunch break until a little past one. I have a patient at one thirty, but it's a beautiful day, and I want to go sit in my car to get some fresh air while I eat a quick lunch. I get in my car and check my phone. I'm more than a little surprised to see that Jordan has texted me:

*Happy Monday, beautiful. I just had to let you know that I can't stop thinking about you. Saturday seems a million hours away, and I'll be missing you until then. Hope you are having a great day!*

I smile at his message and type a quick response:

*And happy Monday to you too! I can't stop thinking about you either. Every minute I get to spend with you is great, but last night was beyond incredible. Counting the hours until Saturday. Missing you.*

I send my message and eat my yogurt. I only have five more minutes until I have to get back to work, and I spend those five minutes thinking about how in the world I can live without Jordan. That thought causes my heart to ache and my eyes to tear up, so I push it away and head back in to work.

The rest of the day is busy but runs smoothly, and I get out the door right on time. When I get home, Noah isn't there. Max is gone, so I know he's taken him out for a walk. I change into my lounging clothes and put together a quick salad to go with the barbeque chicken I had meal prepped for today.

Noah comes back home about twenty minutes after me. He gives me a hug and tells me that Max jumped the highest he's ever seen him jump when he was throwing the Frisbee for him tonight. He tells Max that he deserves some treats, and they disappear into the laundry room where the treat jar is kept.

I mutter under my breath, "My day was fine. And thanks for asking."

I ask Noah if he's ready for dinner, and he says that he needs to change and wash his hands first. I dish up the salad and chicken, open a bottle of water for each of us, and sit down at the table. Noah joins me, and before I can get a single word out, his phone rings.

He looks at the number and says, "Sorry, I have to take this, Kate." And with that he's gone. He goes to his office to take the call, and I decide I'm not waiting for him tonight and start eating. By the time he comes back, I'm on my last bite. He apologizes again.

"Why do they always have to call at dinnertime?" I ask. "I mean, you've been home all day, couldn't they have called earlier?"

He looks annoyed with me and says, "We've been over this, Kate. Sometimes things can't wait, and I have to be available. Is it really that big of a deal?"

I shake my head. There's no point to this. "Sorry. And no, it's not that big of a deal." But it happens at least three or four times a week, and it is a big deal to me. I get up and put my dishes in the dishwasher while he eats and looks at his email. I turn on a recorded episode of a guilty pleasure reality show that I like to watch and curl up on the couch. He tells me he can't concentrate on the email he's trying to read, so he's going to go to his office.

"Sorry, I'll turn this off," I say.

"No, really, I have to send a couple of messages and I might be a while, so go ahead and watch your show." And before he walks away he just has to add, "Not sure how you can stand to watch that crap though." I don't respond and turn my attention back to the TV. He doesn't emerge from his office for over an hour, and by the time he joins me on the couch, it's almost time to go to bed.

\*\*\*

The next two days are the typical routine, except for the fact that Noah says he wants to go out for dinner on Wednesday because he has to leave again the next day. I tell him that sounds nice, and we decide on a Mexican restaurant that's only a couple of miles from our house.

We are having a nice dinner. But I'm finding myself having less and less to say to Noah. And I really don't know if it's because we have drifted apart so much or because my mind is on someone else. I would blame it completely on the fact that

I'm spending time with Jordan except for the fact that I was feeling this way before I ever met him. I just think now it's even more obvious to me because my mind is elsewhere. Not fair to Noah, Kate. Not fair at all!

I'm silently scolding myself when Noah interrupts my thoughts. "You okay? You've seemed so distracted the past couple of weeks. Is there something going on at work?"

I hope my face doesn't show the guilt that I'm feeling inside right now. I manage to sputter, "Um, no, um, I'm sorry. Work is great, and, um, I'm actually going out to dinner with some of the girls on Friday night. It's, um, I guess it's just that you've been gone so much and work just takes up so much of your time." I'm thinking to myself, that's great Kate, how many times did you just say um?!

He doesn't seem to notice. He reaches over, squeezes my hand, and says, "I know. I don't know how to change that right now though. I'm just going to have to suck it up and travel when they need me to. I'm making more money than I ever thought I would, and with the promotion and the increase in pay comes a lot more responsibility."

Then, just before I'm about apologize again, he hits me with, "And I would think you'd be a little more supportive. I mean, it must be nice to only have to work four days a week."

I just nod and say, "Yep, you're right. No one works as hard as you do, Noah. Never mind all the years that I spent working two jobs, going to school, and working weekends. I know that was all before you, but I think I did my time when it comes to working sixty to seventy hours a week."

And just like that, the evening is ruined. We both become silent. He finishes his meal, but I don't feel like eating anymore. The waiter asks me if I'd like a box, and I tell him no thank you. We pay the check and don't speak during the short ride home.

When we get home, I immediately put on my pajamas and brush my teeth. Noah goes to his office and closes the door. I go to bed, and the tears start to fall as soon as I turn off the light. I'm overwhelmed with so many thoughts, and I can't help thinking that it's not like Noah to talk to me like that. Workaholic yes, but he's not mean spirited. It's just not him. And his behavior has been so erratic lately. Like when he came home a couple of weeks ago and surprised me by taking me out to dinner. It was like I had the old Noah back, the man I fell so in love with when we first started dating. I reason with myself that he must be exhausted and tired of traveling, and that's why he's been so moody and distracted. Even though I'm still pissed about the way he talked to me, I resolve to try to be more understanding about his work.

The next thing I know, the alarm is beeping. It's five in the morning, and I need to get up, exercise, and get ready for work. I don't know what time Noah finally came to bed, and he's still sleeping when I leave.

When I get to work, Anna says, "Geez Kate, what's wrong? Your eyes are all puffy, like you've been crying."

"It's really nothing. Noah and I had a little argument last night and I was upset."

"Well, it must have been more than a little argument if you were crying."

"Actually, I'm the one who overreacted. Let's change the subject." Another thing I love about Anna is that she doesn't push.

"Well, you know I'm always here if you want to talk. Now let's get through this day because tomorrow night we are going to drink and look at hot guys in tight pants." Now I'm laughing and tell her that sounds great to me.

I check my phone at twelve thirty, but I don't have any messages. I know that Noah was leaving for the airport at around ten this morning, and a part of me hoped that he would text or leave me a voicemail apologizing for what he said. I decide that I'll give in first and text:

*Hi. Sorry that last night ended badly. I hope that you have a good trip and I'll miss you. I'll take care of Max. Just text me when you can. I know it's tough with the time difference. Love you.*

I finally get a response at five thirty, and it's obvious to me that he's still mad:

*I just landed. Flight was a little bumpy but otherwise fine. Thanks for taking care of Max. Have a good weekend.*

No sorry, no I'll miss you too, and no love you. Thanks a lot, Noah.

\*\*\*

The next morning Anna texts me and says that Yvonne and Mindy are coming to dinner too. Mindy is going to be the designated driver because she has to be up early the next morning and doesn't want to drink. She says that they'll pick me up at five and that we have a reservation. I text her back and thank her for making all the plans. I go and get all my errands done and wash my laundry so I will be free for the rest of the weekend. I have a passing thought about going to the market, but I know that if I was to see Jordan today, I'd want more than just a quick shopping trip. I decide that it's best if I just stick to my plans, and I start getting ready to go out to dinner. I choose a sundress and short denim jacket with my wedge sandals for the evening, and the girls are in my driveway just before five.

When we get to the restaurant, Anna winks at me and says to the hostess, "If Marco is working tonight, we'd like to sit in his section, please." She says that he is working tonight and takes us to a big, circular booth.

After we sit down, I tell Anna, "You are unbelievable." But I'm laughing. And here comes Marco. He's very attractive and has a perfect, bright-white smile, but to say that his pants are tight is an understatement—they look like they're painted on! I'm trying to keep from laughing as Anna stalls him by asking about a dozen questions about the menu, tonight's specials, etc.

We order a pitcher of margaritas, and after he walks away, Anna says, "Well, did I lie?!" I just shake my head and mouth "no" to her. We order a bunch of appetizers to share, and we have no trouble finishing the pitcher of margaritas. Marco is extremely attentive, and we are having a great time. After fighting with Noah, an evening out with the girls is exactly what I needed.

We stay at the restaurant for almost three hours and end up drinking two pitchers of margaritas. We finally decide that we'd better get going, leave Marco a ridiculously big tip, and head out.

The girls drop me off at home, and I'm a little buzzed from the drinks, so I just take Max out in the front yard before bed. Jordan and I had texted earlier in the day and confirmed that I will be at his house at three tomorrow, and I smile thinking about it. I head off to bed and sleep a lot better than I did the night before.

# CHAPTER 29
# 2023

I sleep in a little and don't get up until almost 7:45. After I get done walking Max, I work out and have a granola bar and coffee for breakfast. At about noon I shower and get ready to go to Jordan's house. I'm nervous. Really nervous. We are getting closer physically, and as much as I'm excited about it, I'm also scared. I don't trust my self-control when it comes to him.

And choosing an outfit tonight is really becoming problematic—I want to look pretty but not overtly sexy. After the storm front rolled through last weekend, it was cool for a couple of days, but it's been really warm again since Thursday. And I'll be cooking, so I want to stay cool. I decide on a pair of black and white shorts that are super comfortable because they are a stretchy, pull-on type and the second of the two new shirts I bought when Liz and I went shopping. It's black, sleeveless and a little low cut. I put on my best black bra underneath it, spray on a little perfume, and finally put on my favorite earrings and the wedges I wore last night. I take Max out in the front yard one more time, gather up all the ingredients for dinner, and head out the door at 2:45.

Jordan has the garage open for me as promised, and I park my car like I live there. He meets me at the door before I'm even out of the car and says, "Let me help you." He takes the bags and leaves me to carry only a bottle of wine.

"You didn't have to bring wine too. I always have plenty." I tell him that's sweet but that I wanted to. He puts the bags on the counter and says, "Well, what do we have here?"

I've brought all the ingredients for the seafood pasta. And I chose a highly rated Chardonnay to go with it. He tells me that I did too much and I'm spoiling him and then he pulls me in for a big hug.

"You look so pretty today." I tell him thank you and, as always, he looks great too. He's wearing a fitted white shirt and dark gray shorts. He asks me how my night out with the girls was, and I tell him we had a lot of fun. Then I ask him what he did. He says, "Oh, my buddy and I just went target shooting and had a beer. Typical guy stuff."

"Oh, you like to shoot? I have a little nine millimeter that I've had for years. I got it when I was living alone and I took a safety course to learn how to use it. I used to keep it loaded and near my bed, but now it's in a box in the closet."

He looks impressed and says, "You continue to surprise me. That's cool, Kate. We should go to the shooting range sometime."

I tell him that would be fun because I haven't done it in years. I say that I need to do a little prep work for dinner, and he immediately offers to help. "Not a chance. But you can do one thing for me. Can you just get things out for me as I need them? Right now I need a couple of cutting boards and a couple of small knives."

He jumps up and gets me what I asked for. "I know it's early, but how about I open the wine and we can have a little taste?" I tell him that I like to sip wine while I cook, so I would love that.

He puts on a mix of music, old classics and newer stuff, that's nothing but romantic songs. Then he opens the wine and pours us a taste. I wash my hands, and for the next hour, we talk while I chop basil, shred the parmesan, prep the scallops and shrimp, and juice the lemons.

I put everything in the fridge and take a seat at the island. It's almost four thirty, and I ask him what time he wants to eat. He says he doesn't mind eating a little on the early side because he normally eats dinner by six.

"Well, it takes about forty minutes to pull it all together, so I'll start at about 5:15 then." He says that sounds perfect and we just chat about the shooting range. Then I tell him about the waiter with the painted-on pants from last night.

He laughs and says, "Uh oh, sounds like you girls got a little wild." I tell him that it was fun and that I needed it. He asks me if I had a rough week.

"No, it's just on Wednesday night—" I almost start to tell him about my fight with Noah, but I stop myself. "No, you know what? I want tonight to be fun and stress free so never mind."

He hesitates for a second and then smiles and says, "Me too, Kate."

I realize that the clock says it's 5:25, so I tell him I need to get started. I ask him for a large skillet and pot to cook the pasta in. He gets them out for me, fills the pot with water, and puts it on the stove. I get the seafood ready and transfer it to a plate. Then I make the lemon parmesan sauce and add the seafood to it. After the pasta is cooked, I put everything together, then I top it with more cheese and fresh basil.

While I was cooking, Jordan set the table, closed the blinds, and lit candles. The last thing he does while I'm plating our dinner is dim the lights and refill our wine glasses. We sit down and I tell him that I hope he likes it.

He takes a bite, shakes his head, and says, "That's insanely good! You should give up the whole dental thing and become a chef right now!"

"Okay, I think you're being a little too kind." And he assures me that he's not. I take a bite and say, "Well, it is pretty good."

We enjoy the rest of our meal, and he even has a little more. He tells me the best part is that he will have leftovers for the next couple of days. He puts what's left in the refrigerator, and I insist on cleaning up. I hand wash the pots and pans and put everything else in the dishwasher. While I'm doing that, Jordan wipes off the counters and tops off our wine. I excuse myself and go to the bathroom. I brush, floss, and reapply my lipstick. Jordan is sitting at the dining room table when I come out, and I join him.

We talk for a while and then he says, "Oh, I got something for us. I know you're a healthy eater, and so am I, but these are tiny and so good." He brings out a little box that has four miniature cupcakes in it. "See. They're only like one or two bites. I get them from the bakery on Harrison Street, and they are amazing. Which one do you want?"

I look in the box and debate between the coconut and the lemon. I choose the coconut, and he chooses the red velvet. I take a tiny bite, and he's right; it's amazing.

After we finish, he asks, "Would you dance with me, Kate?" I tell him I would love to. "Can't Help Falling in Love," which is one of my favorites, is playing low in the background when he takes my hand and pulls me close to him. We are as close as we can get, cheek to cheek and swaying slowly to the music. He moves his head so he can look me right in the eyes.

"I'm so glad I bumped into you, literally, in the market that day. I love spending time with you. And you're perfect, except for one thing." I didn't expect that, and I'm afraid the next thing he's going to say is that I'm perfect except for the fact that I'm already taken. But instead he smiles and says, "Except for the fact that you have a little bit of frosting on your lip."

I roll my eyes and say, "Oh, great," and immediately bring my hand up to wipe it off.

He halts my wrist before I can and says, "How about you let me get that for you?"

I feel like everything's in slow motion, and I just nod my approval. And then it's happening. His lips are on mine. And this man knows how to kiss. It's as passionate as a kiss can be but soft and perfect. He doesn't try to force his tongue in my mouth, and he's not slobbering all over me.

I kiss him back, and it's the beginning of a two-hour-long make-out session. We continue to kiss and slow dance for two more songs, and then he asks me if I'd like to move over to the couch where we'll be more comfortable. I feel like I've lost the power of speech and just nod in agreement again.

When we get to the couch, I lean back in the corner at an angle and stretch my legs out in front of me. The couch is a big sectional with a chaise and double ottoman, so there's more than enough room for him to climb in right beside me and sit the same way. We immediately start kissing again and his hands are all over me. He's gentle when he touches me, and he's not even close to trying to touch me underneath my bra. He's just softly stroking my hair, my sides, my stomach, and all the way down and back up my legs. I'm touching him the same way.

We move on to kissing in other places too. I kiss his neck like I did a few days ago, and he sighs with approval. Only this time I don't want to stop. I lift up his shirt and kiss his chest, all along the sides of his ribcage and stomach. He's flinching, and I ask him if he wants me to stop.

He looks at me like I'm crazy and says, "Are you kidding? No way, it's just that ticklish thing—I'll get past it. It feels incredible, so please don't stop." I smile and continue with what I'm doing. Pretty soon he stops flinching and he's just breathing heavily and sighing. I kiss his thighs, make my way down his calves and all the way back up again.

He pulls me up next to him and says, "Your turn." I'm suddenly self-conscious and, without a word, he gets up and turns the lights off so all we have is candlelight. It amazes me how we've only known each other a few weeks and he's able to read me the way he does. He slides up next to me and says, "Now, where was I? Oh yeah, I was about to kiss every inch of you."

Just hearing that makes me feel like I'm on fire inside, and I don't think it can get any better until I feel his soft lips on my neck. He continues all the way down my body, and when he gets to my ankles, he softly strokes them with little circles and then kisses them over and over as lightly as he can. Then he kisses his way all the way back up my legs again. I tell him that I don't think I can take much more and we should take a break.

He smiles and says, "I don't want to, but okay, just a short one. I think I can wait a few minutes to torture you some more." We catch our breath for about ten minutes, sip a little more wine, and go right back at it.

We've come up for air for at least the fourth time when I look at the clock and see that it's almost eleven. I tell him that as much as I don't want to, I should go soon. I tell him that I'm going to get an Uber again and say, "I think next time I come over, I'll just get a ride to begin with."

"That works. I'll just come get you next time." Just hearing him say that, without hesitation, makes me feel cared for and makes me realize how much I've been missing that so much lately.

While I wait for my ride, we kiss and hug in the kitchen. Before I leave, we decide to go to the shooting range the next day. He says that the range is outdoors and we'll be far away from anyone else who might be there. I tell him that sounds like fun. Then he says he'll pick me at the doughnut shop tomorrow at eleven.

My ride is waiting, so I give him one last kiss and tell him I'll see him tomorrow.

When I get home, I let Max out and get ready for bed. It's after midnight by the time I'm done. I check my phone, and I see that Noah texted me about two hours ago:

*Hi. I'm sure you're in bed. Hope you had a good day and that you had fun with the girls last night. Busy day today. Unless there are any delays, my flight gets in at 3:58 tomorrow afternoon. Can you pick me up? Thanks.*

His message seems like he's not as angry as he was when he left, but still no "love you" at the end. I'll have to leave by a little past three to pick him up tomorrow, so that doesn't leave much time with Jordan and I'm disappointed.

I lie down in my bed and replay Jordan and me on the couch over and over again in my mind until I fall asleep.

# CHAPTER 30
# 2008

I know that my marriage to Alex is not going well at all, and I'm mad at myself for ever going through with it in the first place. He's so unpredictable—sometimes he's sweet and loving, but he can literally change overnight and be verbally abusive the next day. Lately I've been avoiding sex with him with excuses, and we've only slept together a couple of times in the past few months. I can't even believe that I ever enjoyed being intimate with him, but there were times when I did—those times always being when he was going through a sweet, loving phase. Until he made sure I would never enjoy being with him again.

We've been married for almost seven months now, and today is his birthday. It's a Saturday, so I make plans for the evening. I plan on taking him out for a great dinner; I bake him a cake from scratch and get a new dress to wear to dinner. I've also decided that I'm going to make an effort to be intimate with him. I guess I feel like I'm just not ready to give up on the marriage yet.

I get up early and make his favorite, French toast. When he gets up, I start singing "Happy Birthday to you…," but he stops me.

"Please don't. I'm not happy about being a year older, so just don't, ok?"

I laugh and say, "Oh, come on, you're only twenty-six! You should want to celebrate."

He looks angry and says, "Are you making fun of me? If I don't want you to sing to me, then you should just shut up."

I'm upset by how he just snapped at me, but I try to salvage the day and say, "No, I would never make fun of you. I'm sorry, and you're right, if you don't want me to sing to you, then I won't. Um, I did make you French toast, if you want some."

"Geez, I'm sorry. I guess I'm just in a bad mood. Yeah, I'd love some."

I was going to put a candle in it for him but decide to scrap that idea. We eat breakfast and his mood seems to improve, so I tell him I've made dinner plans for tonight. He says that's fine but right now he's going to hang out with his buddy and play some video games to "celebrate" his birthday.

I try to keep a positive attitude and get ready for the evening. When he gets home, we get changed and head out to dinner. He says nothing about my dress, so I say, "I bought this dress to wear for you tonight. What do you think?"

"It's nice, but do you always have to wear black? There are other colors, you know." I can't hide the hurt look on my face and he tries to backpedal, "I mean, it looks fine. I just like seeing you in bright colors, that's all."

"Thanks, I'll try to remember that in the future."

We get to the restaurant and actually start to have a good time. We have a couple of great steaks, and I tell him not to order dessert because I've got cake waiting for him at home. We go home and I get the cake out of the fridge. It's his favorite, carrot cake. We each have a piece and he tells me it was great.

I say that I want to get out of my dress and put on something more comfortable, and he goes and turns on the TV. Still having second thoughts, I decide to keep trying and put on a short, satin nightie. I choose my black one at first, but after the comment about my dress, I decide on my red one instead. I come out of the bedroom and say, "So, here's another present for you." He doesn't even look up from the TV, so I walk over and sit on the arm of the chair next to him.

He finally looks at me and says, "What are you doing?"

"I thought I'd give you one last birthday present." I'm shocked to see that he looks mad, and I mean really mad. "What's wrong?" What he says to me will be burned in my memory forever.

"I can't believe you think I want to have sex with you. You don't do anything for me. You're skinny and pale, and I hate your blonde hair and blue eyes. I like women who have dark hair and brown eyes. There's not one single thing that's attractive about you. Not one."

I'm so shocked that I can't speak for at least thirty seconds. I start to cry and finally say, "I can't believe you just said that to me. Then why did you marry me? And why did you ever sleep with me in the first place?"

He looks at me, smirks, and says, "Because I'm always thinking of someone else." Then he just starts laughing. Less than fifteen minutes ago, we were having a good evening, and I can't understand what makes him spiral like this out of nowhere.

I quietly go to bed, and the next day he acts like nothing happened. When he's in the shower, his phone beeps and I look at it. It's his ex-girlfriend, who he had left me for in the past. The message just says hi and wishes him a nice day, but I can see that she also messaged him right around the time we got home last night. I read that message too, and it says, "Happy Birthday. Are you thinking about how we celebrated your birthday two years ago? I am! XOXOXO."

And that explains everything. Guess what she looks like? Tan, dark brown hair, and brown eyes. I wouldn't doubt it if they still message and talk to each other frequently. I didn't want to risk getting caught looking through his phone, so I put it back where I found it and leave the house for the day.

It's only a couple months later when he punches me, and I decide to divorce him on the spot. I'm still ashamed that it took something so violent to make me wake up and get out of a horrible situation that I should have never let myself get into in the first place.

# CHAPTER 31
# 2023

I wake up at exactly seven, and I have a sickening feeling as soon as I open my eyes. I usually don't remember all the details from my dreams, but this time I do. I dreamed about Alex and how he put me down and abused me. I haven't thought about that in a long time, and I don't like thinking about it now. I don't know why I dreamed about him. Unless it was because of what Jordan and I did last night.

No matter how much therapy I've had in my life, I don't think I'll ever have 100 percent confidence in my looks and my body. My dad, Alex, and a lot of other people took that confidence from me, and it's a tough road to try to get it back.

I shower, put on jeans, a T-shirt, and a baseball cap. Then I walk up to the doughnut shop to meet Jordan. When I get in the car, he greets me with good morning and a quick kiss. We are just looking at each other, smiling, and then he takes my hands in his and says, "Before we go anywhere, I want to tell you how much I enjoyed last night. Touching you was incredible, and being touched by you was indescribable. I think I've got a crush on you, Kate."

We both laugh, and I say, "A crush, huh? Well, I think it's more than a crush for me. I can't put into words how incredible last night was. You are amazing, Jordan." He tells me thank you, gives me one more kiss, and we drive to the gun range.

We shoot for over an hour. He does a lot better than I do, but for being out of practice, I don't do too badly. He assures me that I'm a "badass," and we agree that it was a lot of fun and need to do it again sometime soon.

We drive back to his house, and I have about an hour before I'll have to go home and then get to the airport to pick up Noah. We go inside, sit at the kitchen island, and drink a bottle of water. He asks me what my week looks like, and I tell him that Monday is always my busiest day, but it should be a pretty average week for me. I ask him about his week, and he tells me that it should be an average week for him too.

Then he says, "I hope that after Thursday, it will be anything but average. I need to ask you something." I'm not sure what's coming next but I tell him to ask away. He says, "Okay, here goes. How about we go away next weekend? I was thinking we could drive to the northern part of Arizona. The hiking is great, and there are all these small towns that have a bunch of shops and restaurants. We could just enjoy the weekend and not have to worry about being out in public together. If you aren't comfortable with that, I totally understand, so no pressure. What do you think?"

I don't have to think about it. I nod enthusiastically and say, "Yes, that sounds amazing. Count me in." He looks relieved, hugs me, and says, "We will have a great time, Kate. I'll make the arrangements, and we can just leave from here on Friday morning."

I tell him that sounds perfect but now, unfortunately, I have to get going. He looks disappointed for a few seconds but says, "I'm not happy that you have to go, but knowing I get you all to myself for an entire weekend makes it a little more bearable." I tell him that I feel the same. He drives me back to the doughnut shop and after a few more goodbye kisses, I reluctantly get out of the car.

When I get home, I tidy up the house a bit, take Max on a quick walk, and drive to the airport. I'm dreading seeing Noah. Since the fight the night before he left, we have barely spoken. But when he gets in the car, he says, "Hey, babe. How are you? I missed you."

Hmm, I didn't expect that. Not that I expected him to be nasty to me or give me the silent treatment, because that's not how Noah behaves at all, but I didn't expect him to be so glad to see me. I say, "Yeah, I missed you too. How was your flight home?"

He tells me that the flight was fine and then immediately asks me what I did over the weekend. I tell him about going out with the girls on Friday and say that the rest of the weekend was just the usual errands and housework. I sigh and add, "Look, I don't like what happened before you left."

Before I can say anything else, he says, "I know. Me too. I was angry, and I shouldn't have talked to you like that. I'm sorry." I tell him that I'm sorry too. After we both apologize, neither one of us is talking, and after five minutes of silence, I turn on the radio.

When we get home, he does his usual—drops his bag in the office and plays with Max. I used to complain about him not unpacking until a day or two later, but he's just not a person that likes to unpack the same day he gets home. Whenever I get home from a trip, I unpack and do all of my laundry immediately. I used to unpack his bag for him, but he told me that even though he really appreciates it, he'd just rather wait a day or two and doesn't want me to feel like I need to take care of it. So I stopped doing it, and I don't say anything about it anymore.

He says, "It's early. Do you want to go out and grab a bite to eat?" When he talks about food, my stomach growls and I suddenly realize that I haven't eaten since I had toast at around nine this morning.

"Sure. That sounds good. Where do you want to go?" He suggests a casual steak place that's only about fifteen minutes from home, and I tell him that's fine with me.

We go to dinner and it's nice. But that's it. Just nice. I keep thinking, Shouldn't I want to grab him and kiss him? Whenever I'm with Jordan, I constantly want to grab him and kiss him. I tell myself that comparing the two situations is not fair at all.

We get into our lounging clothes when we get home, and he asks me if I want to watch TV. I want to try to connect with him a little more, even though every time I've tried for the past year he hasn't responded. I tell myself not to dwell on that, to be fair to Noah and keep trying.

I say, "No, not really. Why don't we sit at the dining room table and talk? I'll pour us a glass of wine, ok?"

"Ok." He sounds a little unsure.

I get the wine and dim the lights a little. As soon as I sit down, he says, "So the practice manager at the first clinic I got sent to this time was such a dick! He actually told me that he'd have to check and see if the doctor had time to meet with me. Can you believe that?! I told him that I didn't need him to check and see because I have an appointment—"

"Sorry to interrupt you," I cut him off. "But can we talk about something else besides work? I mean, you worked all weekend and I have to work all week. Can we just try to enjoy a little time together?"

He looks irritated, sighs, and says, "Sure, I guess. What do you want to talk about then?"

"Well, I didn't have anything specific in mind." But that's not true. I'd like to talk to him about a lot of things; his mood swings, his hot and cold behavior toward me, the fact that our marriage has no intimacy… But he looks annoyed, so I don't say anything else.

He just shrugs his shoulders, and now I'm the one who's irritated. I try to lighten the mood and tell him about the waiter with the tight pants and how funny it was. He barely cracks a smile and says, "Sounds like you guys had fun."

Neither one of us says a word for at least fifteen seconds. I decide to push on and give it one more try. I say, "Yeah, the pants aside, the guy was pretty good looking, and Yvonne was flirting hard."

"Well, was he good looking?"

"I guess. But you're much better looking." I reach across the table and take his hand.

He just says, "Thanks." The next thing I know, he's turned away from me, petting the dog with his free hand and throwing a toy for him.

I let go of his hand and say, "Let's just watch a little TV and go to bed."

"Okay, I'm going to take Max out first." I just nod and stay in my chair.

I feel like I'm going to cry and I don't want to. I fight back the tears and decide I'm just going to go ahead and go to bed. I'm reading when he comes in the bedroom. He asks me if I'd mind turning off the light—he's exhausted and wants to get some sleep. I tell him that's fine, turn off the light, and try to sleep. I toss and turn, and the last time I look at the clock, it's after one.

I'm not ready for the day when the alarm goes off at five. As much as I don't want to, I get out of bed and slowly start my day. Noah's still sleeping when I leave for work.

\*\*\*

It's a typical busy Monday, and when I get home, Noah is in the office doing something for work. I start boiling water for pasta and put some garlic bread in the oven.

When dinner is almost ready, he comes out of the office and says, "Yum, I thought I smelled garlic bread."

He gives me a quick hug, and we do the usual "How was your day?" before sitting down to eat. I ask him where he'll be traveling to this weekend. He says that he's not sure if it's going to be Texas or Tennessee this time and they're going to let him know tomorrow. Then he says, "Oh yeah, speaking of tomorrow, Joe and Barb invited us to come over for drinks and appetizers tomorrow at six thirty. Okay?"

Joe works with Noah, and he's really nice, but I'm not Barb's biggest fan—and Noah knows it. But, again, I tell myself I need to keep trying. "Sure, we can. But you have to work at the office on Wednesday, right? You sure you want to go out the night before?"

He says that we won't stay out late, and he'll make sure we're home before ten.

The next night I pick out a long sundress to wear and we make the short drive to Joe's house that's less than five miles away. There are four other couples there, and I'm grateful I don't have to spend an evening where the only other woman I have to talk to is Barb. Noah is charming and talkative all night. He frequently has his arm around me, and all I can think is why can't he be like this at home?!

I'm getting tired. I look at my watch and see that it's 10:20. Noah is deep into a conversation about work (what else?) with Joe. I walk over and say, "Sorry to interrupt, but we should be going soon, honey."

Noah says, "Yeah, sure, just give me a minute."

He immediately launches back into the work conversation with Joe, and I just go and make a little small talk with the only other couple that's still here. I'm getting increasingly annoyed, and at 11:10 I finally interrupt one more time, but before I can say anything, Joe says, "Geez, I'm sorry, Kate. I didn't realize what time it was. You have to work tomorrow, don't you? Noah, take this beautiful woman home."

Noah looks irritated and says, "Yeah, I guess we should go. Thanks for everything." I tell Joe and Barb thank you, say goodbye to the other couple, and head to the car while Noah is still saying goodbye at the door.

He gets in the car, and I'm shocked when he says, "Don't you think you were being a little rude, Kate? I mean, I know you don't really care for Barb, but you didn't need to be rude to Joe."

I'm pissed off now. "First of all, I wasn't rude to Joe. Second of all, you were the one being rude. To me. You promised me that we would be home before ten, and here it is almost eleven thirty. You would still be there if I hadn't asked you to leave. Twice! Funny how you're always too tired or too busy working to talk to me, but you're a total chatterbox when it comes to your work friends!"

He glares at me, and now he's mad. He shakes his head and says, "Well, maybe I'd want to talk to you more if you were interested in what I have to say!"

I can't believe he just said that, and I'm really raising my voice when I say, "Are you kidding me? How interested can I be when all you ever talk about is *work*?! Oh and Max! Maybe if you talked to me about something else once in a while, I'd be interested!"

He yells back, "Like what?!"

And before I can stop myself, I shout, "I don't know. Life, our future, what our plans are, places we'd like to go, things we'd like to do together. And how about sex? Actually, that's a great topic! We should talk about how you haven't touched me in over six months!"

The words tumble out before I can stop them, and they're met with deafening silence. Noah shifts the car into gear and starts driving. When we get home, he gets out of car and slams the door, leaving me sitting in the passenger seat. I wait a minute before going into the house. He's putting Max on his leash, so I just get ready for bed while he goes out.

The next morning he's already up and has walked Max by the time I get out of the shower. Without looking at me he says, "I've got to go to work, see you later."

Without looking at him either, I just say, "Bye."

For the second night in a row, I didn't get much sleep, and I'm feeling it today. Anna sees me right after I get to work and says, "What's going on with you? You look like shit today."

I smile and say, "Gee, thanks Anna."

She laughs and says, "Sorry, but you do." Then she looks serious. "What's going on, Kate?" I feel the tears coming, but it's too late. I start to cry. She didn't expect that. She grabs me by my shoulders, guides me into the X-ray room, and shuts the door. She hands me a bunch of tissues and says, "Talk to me. What's wrong? Why are you crying?"

I desperately want to tell her. I want to tell her everything. I want to tell her about my problems with Noah. I want to tell her about Jordan. But I just can't. I say, "I don't know. I guess Noah and I are just having a hard time. He's been working so much, and we just feel…disconnected."

She tells me she's sorry and assures me that when his schedule gets back to normal, things will get better. Everything I would expect a good friend to say. Then she looks me in the eyes and says, "Are you sure that's it? There isn't anything else bothering you?"

Damn. She knows me well. I assure her there's nothing else and wonder to myself if there will ever come a day when I will tell her about Jordan. I say, "I'm done now. I need to dry my eyes and get to my patient."

She hugs me and tells me that she's always here for me whenever I need her. And I know she is.

I check my phone at lunch. No text from Noah. But there is one from Jordan:

*Hello, sexy. The arrangements have been made—and I might have a surprise or two for you. I booked us two deluxe rooms, side by side, at the Mountain View Inn for Friday and Saturday night. I hope you are having a great day. The weekend can't get here soon enough! Miss you.*

I'm impressed that he booked us in separate rooms without me having to ask, and I respond:

*Hi, handsome. That sounds wonderful, and I can't wait. I hope you are having a good day, mine is fine. Miss you more!*

I text Liz. I haven't seen her since we had lunch and went shopping, which is longer than we usually go without seeing each other. She's been busy. She was on a family trip two weeks ago and at her daughter, Tara's, cheerleading competition last weekend.

*Hi, friend! I feel like I haven't seen you in a million years! How about dinner tomorrow night?*

She responds almost immediately:

*I know! It's just been ridiculously busy and I'm exhausted. I would love to go to dinner, but we are leaving to go to Tara's last competition tomorrow night. It's more than an hour and a half away, and we didn't want to have to get up at the crack of dawn to drive there Friday morning. It's the finals, so it will be all weekend, and we won't be home until Sunday night. Hey, why don't you come with us?! I would love it, and I know that Tara would love it if her Aunt Kate was there!*

Now I'm thinking about what to tell her. I've been to a lot of Tara's cheerleading competitions in the past, and we always have a great time. What comes to mind should have come to mind before—Max! I hadn't thought about what I'm going to do with the dog while I'm gone this weekend. Shit!

*I would love to go, but Noah is on week four of his weekends of working out of town, and I have to be home to take care of Max. I could try to get a dog sitter, but I doubt that I can on such short notice. Sorry!*

She responds immediately:

*Oh, that's right. I forgot Noah will be gone. Can we do dinner tonight? I don't want to wait another week or two before I see you again!*

I text her back and tell her that we can definitely do dinner tonight, and we make plans to meet a deli close to her house right after work. I text Noah to let him know, and he responds:

*Okay. I'm going to Tennessee this weekend, by the way. Flight leaves at 9:15 tomorrow morning.*

Before I go back to work for the afternoon, I call the dog sitter that Noah and I have used in the past. She tells me that she's already booked for the weekend but gives me numbers of two other people that she knows and recommends. I call the first one, but he's booked too. Shit! Thank goodness the second one is available, and I make arrangements for her to come by tomorrow evening when I get off work so she can meet Max and get the garage door code.

I meet Liz for dinner after work, and the first thing I say is, "Sorry I look like the walking dead. I didn't sleep well last night." She asks me why, and I say, "Well, since Mark got to be the butthole last time, it was Noah's turn this week." She rolls her eyes, we both laugh, and she asks me what he did.

I tell her about the fight we had last night, leaving out the part about us not having sex for the past six months, and she says, "You were perfectly justified in getting upset; he was being rude to you!"

I interrupt and ask her, "Honestly, do you think I was being unreasonable?" She assures me, "Not at all. I know you. You don't like to be out late when you have to work the next day. You get up so early in the morning, and he should appreciate the fact that you agreed to go at all!" Then she adds, "Butthole!" And we both laugh. I tell her I don't want to talk about it anymore and we enjoy the rest of our time together.

When we're getting ready to leave the restaurant, I say, "I wish that I could go this weekend. Please tell Tara that I wish her luck and I know that they're going to win!" She promises to tell her, and we agree to meet up for dinner again in a couple of weeks.

When I get home, Noah is watching TV with Max in his lap.

"Hi," I say. "How was your day?"

He responds, "Fine," without taking his eyes off the TV.

I try one more time. "I think we should talk about last night. I don't like you leaving tomorrow with both of us upset."

He finally looks at me and says, "I'm not upset, Kate, and I really don't want to talk about it. We were both wrong, and let's just leave it at that."

Even though I tell him that's fine, I'm mad all over again! Lately he just sweeps everything under the rug and there's not even an attempt at an apology.

***

Early the next morning, he's packing his bag again, getting ready to go to the airport. Now's my chance to tell him I'll be away. "Oh, I forgot to tell you. I'm going with Liz and Mark to Tara's cheerleading competition this weekend. We're leaving tomorrow morning, and I won't be home until Sunday night. I already called and arranged for the pet sitter to take care of Max."

He says, "Well, okay, I guess. I just wish you would have told me before this morning."

I sigh and say, "Noah, I'm sorry, okay, I meant to tell you Tuesday night, but we had that fight, and it just slipped my mind. If you don't want me to go, then I won't." I say it, but I'm thinking that there's no way I'm not going out of town this weekend.

"Well, I guess since you arranged to have the pet sitter come, it will be fine." I assure him that I will check in with the sitter at least twice a day and I can come back if anything unforeseen happens. He nods and says "Okay, I've got to get going, Kate. Love you." I tell him I love him too, and after a quick hug for me and about ten hugs and kisses for Max, he leaves.

Jordan and I text during my lunch break and decide to leave at ten thirty the next morning. After I get home from work, the pet sitter comes over. She's a young girl, full of energy, and Max takes right to her. She asks if she can take him on a quick walk so he will be used to her putting him on the leash.

After she walks him, I give her the garage code, my phone number, and our veterinarian's phone number and pay her with a check. She says she will plan on coming over three times a day and assures me that she will send me pictures every time she's here.

After she leaves I see that I've missed a text from Noah letting me know that he had dinner and just got back to his hotel room. He says he's exhausted and he's going to go to bed. I text him back and tell him that I'm going to go to bed early tonight too and that I'll text him tomorrow.

I get my bag packed, and I'm in bed and asleep before nine o'clock.

# CHAPTER 32
# 2023

When I get to Jordan's house, he's ready to go. We make a quick stop for bagels and coffee, and then we hit the road. My bad mood that I've been in for the past two days is immediately replaced with excitement and anticipation. We listen to music and conversation flows effortlessly, like it always seems to for us.

I keep trying to get him to tell me what the surprises are, and he smiles and says, "Now if I told you, then you wouldn't be surprised, would you? I asked you to bring a dressy outfit, a casual outfit and hiking shoes, and those are the only clues you're getting." I relent and wonder what he could have in store for me. The drive takes a little over four hours, and I enjoy every minute.

The hotel is beautiful, but we aren't able to check into our rooms for another hour. We leave our bags and go over to a couple of the little shops right next door to kill time.

It's a little past four thirty when we get to our rooms, and Jordan tells me that we have dinner reservations at six. He lets me know we are going to get a ride to the restaurant, about ten minutes from the hotel.

I smile and say, "Sounds good. I need to freshen up and get changed. How about you pick me up at five thirty?" He tells me he'll be at my door at exactly five thirty.

He had told me that we were going somewhere really nice for dinner tonight, so I unpack my dress and heels, along with the rest of my clothes and toiletries. I washed my hair this morning but didn't do much with it beyond that, so I use my flat iron to make loose waves. After I finish with my hair, I touch up my makeup and get dressed. I put on my burgundy red dress that falls just above my knees and has a pretty low neckline. Then I put on my high heels, a pair of sparkly drop earrings, and a thin silver necklace to complete everything.

I spray on some perfume and take a last look in the full-length mirror. The cut of the dress is flattering, and it's one of my favorites. I'm lost in thought about how long it's been since I really dressed up like this when I hear a knock at the door—at five thirty on the dot.

When I open the door, I'm speechless. Jordan's wearing black pants and a black sport coat. He has a white dress shirt underneath the jacket with the top two buttons undone. It's a dressy look but still casual because he's not wearing a tie, which, I think, would have been too much. Chalk up another point for this guy—he knows how to dress. He looks like he just stepped out of a magazine, and I feel my heart start to race. All I can say is "Wow! You look so good!"

He shakes his head and says, "Me? What about you? Let me look at you." I step back and do a slow turn for him. He gives me a little whistle and says, "You are drop-dead gorgeous! Every guy in the place is going to be so jealous of me!"

I tell him that I think he's being a little over the top, and he becomes serious, "Kate. Honestly. How can you not know how beautiful you are? I swear that someday I'm going to make you believe it." I thank him but silently wish him good luck on that one. Then we share a quick hug and head out for the evening.

The restaurant is beautiful. All the tables are aglow from soft candlelight and crystal chandeliers. There are black tablecloths, comfy chairs with thick velvet cushions, polished hardwood floors, and the wait staff are all dressed in black tie. Our waiter asks us to follow him, and as we're walking across the restaurant, Jordan squeezes my hand and whispers, "Surprise number one."

The waiter opens a set of double doors and takes us out to a private balcony. The table is the same as the tables inside, only smaller, more intimate. There is a single taper candle in the middle, we are surrounded by glowing lanterns all around the perimeter of the balcony, and there's a hidden speaker playing soft music. To say it's beautiful is an understatement because it's something straight out of a movie. For the second time tonight, I'm rendered speechless.

Jordan pulls my chair out for me, and after I sit down I finally manage to say, "I can't believe you did this. It's so beautiful that I can't even put it into words. Thank you."

He smiles and says, "I'm glad you approve. And you're more than welcome, Kate. This weekend is about spoiling you, and I'm going to enjoy every minute of it." The waiter comes back, and Jordan asks if I'd like a glass of Pinot Noir. I tell him that sounds perfect.

When the waiter returns with our wine, he's carrying a long stem rose and says, "This is for the beautiful lady." I know that Jordan arranged this too, and all I can do is shake my head and thank him.

Everything on the menu sounds incredible, and I finally decide on the grilled halibut with asparagus. Jordan orders the ribeye with a baked potato, and we decide to share the crab-stuffed mushrooms to start. The mushrooms arrive and they are delicious. We hold hands, sip our wine, and talk about how nice it would be to come here a few times a year. Our entrées are fantastic, and we both eat every bite. We order a second glass of wine, and the waiter returns with dessert. It's a beautiful lemon and coconut cake that's dusted with powdered sugar and surrounded by raspberries.

Jordan says, "I know you don't eat dessert very often, but it's small, and I thought it might be a nice way to end our meal." I tell him that I'm all for it. My entrée was very healthy, so I definitely have a little room left for dessert.

Jordan encourages me to take the first bite, and after I do, I say, "Oh, come on. Nothing should be that good!" Then I spoon up another bite and feed it to him. We agree that it's the best dessert we've ever had, and we have no trouble finishing it. We linger over our wine for another thirty minutes and, even though we don't want to, we decide it's time to go.

When we get back to the hotel, I say, "If you walk me to my door, I just might invite you in." Jordan smiles and tells me that's an offer he would never refuse. As soon as we shut the door behind us, he pulls me to him and kisses me, in that urgent but incredibly soft way he does. I melt into him, and I don't ever want to stop.

He tells me that he'd like to go to his room and change clothes, and I tell him I'd like to do the same. I haven't worn heels in quite some time and my feet are a little sore. I put on a pair of jogger pants, a T-shirt, and my flip flops; then I brush my teeth and put my hair in a ponytail. When Jordan comes back, he's dressed pretty similar to me. He tells me that I'm just as beautiful now as I was ten minutes ago, and I marvel at how he knows exactly what to say.

What happens next surprises me. There's a large window showcasing a beautiful mountain view and a small table and chairs at the end of the room, and Jordan asks me if I'd like to sit there and talk. We end up talking for hours. He tells me more about his childhood, college, and talks a little more about Rachel. I end up talking about my childhood illnesses, my dysfunctional family, and more about my past relationships.

What surprises me is how I'm opening up to him. I'm more than embarrassed about my dysfunctional family and how I let a lot of men in my past treat me, and I really didn't think I'd tell him a lot of things I'm telling him tonight. I realize how long I've been talking and say, "Sorry. I didn't mean to unload like that." Then I try to lighten the mood, laugh, and say, "Pretty scary, huh? You should run out of here and never look back."

He doesn't crack a smile and says, "Look at me, Kate. The way some people have treated you in your life is horrific. Those men who abused you and cheated on you—well, they're not men. They're insecure narcissists who took out their feelings of inadequacy on you, the person who was trying to love them. That is such a cowardly thing to do and, if anything, you should just pity them. Be proud of how you've risen above all that. You are amazing, and I'm lucky that you are part of my life."

By the time he's done speaking, I have tears in my eyes, and all I can say in response is, "I'm the lucky one, Jordan."

He gets up and walks over to me, and we hug for what seems like a very long time. Then he releases me and says, "Okay, now I want to you to get good sleep because we are going to have a great day tomorrow. If it's all right with you, I'll be here at ten, we'll have brunch and go on a hike, and then I have another surprise for you tomorrow night. I tell him that sounds perfect. He gives me one last quick kiss and goes to his room. I wash my face, get in bed, and sleep like a baby.

\*\*\*

The next morning we go to brunch at the hotel, and Jordan tells me to make sure I get enough to eat because it might be late when we get dinner tonight. We order eggs benedict, a huge Belgium waffle, and a half pot of coffee. We share the food and head out to go on a two-hour hike.

It's a beautiful day, and the scenery is gorgeous. I take a lot of pictures, and when we get to the end of the hike, even though I normally say no to selfies, I pull Jordan close to me for a picture. After we take multiple shots, we get in the car and head back toward the hotel. We park the car and decide to walk through a few more of the shops.

We find a shop called Mitchell's Treasures that has all kinds of olive oils and spices on one side and homemade candles, lotions, and hand soaps on the other side. We split up, and I pick up a couple of different olive oils, a big three-wick blueberry pie candle, a candle lighter, and a couple of hand soaps. When I get up to the register, Jordan is already standing there with a bag.

I ask him what he bought, and he says, "Hmm, I think I'll keep that a secret for now. Maybe I'll tell you later." I'm confused as to why he won't tell me what he bought, but I'm thinking he probably bought something for me, and he wants to give it to me later. He looks at his watch and says, "Are you ready to head back to the hotel? It's a little after three, and our ride will be there at four thirty to pick us up. Dress casual and bring a jacket tonight, okay?"

I say, "Okay, but where are we going?"

He just smiles and says, "Surprise number two, Kate."

When we get back to the hotel, I jump in the shower because I got a little sweaty from the hike. After I shower I fix my makeup and hair. I decide to wear a pair of casual black pants, a short-sleeve black and white top, and my favorite black wedge sandals. I put on a pair of small diamond earrings and grab my denim jacket. I see that the pet sitter has texted me twice showing me pictures of her walking Max. I text her a quick thank you, and then I text Noah:

*Hi. I hope your trip is going well. Competition will probably be over in an hour or so. We are going to dinner afterward, so I just wanted to tell you goodnight.*

I debate on saying "love you," but I'm still mad about the way things went before he left, so I don't. I'm feeling guilty about lying though, and I try to push that thought away.

My thoughts, gratefully, are interrupted by Jordan knocking on my door. When I open it, he says, "I know it's getting redundant, so I'll just say that you are gorgeous."

He's wearing dark-washed jeans and an untucked, light blue button-down shirt. The shirt makes his eyes look even bluer, and all I can manage to say is, "So handsome."

He says, "Our ride awaits," and we head down to the lobby. When we get to the doors, I can't believe what I'm seeing. There's a limo, and the driver is waiting, holding the door open for us.

I look at Jordan and say, "You didn't really do that, did you?"

He just smiles and says, "Yes, it's all part of the surprise."

"Wait a minute, I thought this was the surprise. There's more?" He just smiles and steers me toward the car. We drive for over thirty minutes, and I'm thinking to myself that it looks like we're out in the middle of nowhere, and then I see it—a hot air balloon!

I'm practically jumping up and down in my seat and say, "Really? No way!"

"Well, when we went to see the balloons, I felt bad that we had to cut it short. I remember you telling me that taking a ride in one was on your bucket list, and I've never been in one either, so we are going to take a sunset ride tonight." I throw my arms around him and give him a big hug.

We get in the balloon, and the next thing I know, we're in the air going past the most beautiful red rock mountains I've ever seen. Again, it's like something straight out of a movie, and I can't believe I'm actually living it. The pilot says, "Champagne?" We tell him that sounds great, he pours, and we clink our glasses together. We start floating down just as the sun is setting, and it's so perfect. The limo takes us back to the hotel, and I've thanked Jordan at least ten times by the time we arrive. He keeps telling me that I don't have to thank him, but I can't seem to stop.

When we get to my room, he asks me if I'm hungry and I tell him I'm really not. Brunch was a big meal, and I don't think I really want dinner. I say that maybe we can just get a little snack later. He says he feels the same way. I ask him if he wants to come in and promise him we will have much happier conversations tonight.

"Yes, of course, but let me go to my room first. I want to grab something."

I look at him and he's smirking. I say, "What are you up to now?"

And his only response is, "Be right back."

I go into my room and decide to light the candle I bought at the shop today. Within a minute the room starts to smell exactly like blueberry pie baking. I use the bathroom and run a brush through my hair. Jordan is back, and he has the bag from Mitchell's in his hand, along with a bottle of wine, an opener, and two glasses.

"Are you going to tell me what you bought now?"

He smiles and says, "Yes, but first of all, that candle smells amazing! I'm going to have to go back to that store and get one of those. And this is what I bought today." He pulls a small bottle out of the bag: vanilla cinnamon massage oil. He says, "I thought I could give you a massage tonight, if you would be okay with that."

This guy can't be real. Maybe I'm asleep and I've dreamed the whole thing! "Jordan, you have spoiled me so much already. That sounds wonderful, but I'd like to reciprocate."

He hesitates for a moment and then says, "I promise that I'll let you reciprocate, but not tonight, maybe next weekend." I push and say I'd like it to be tonight, and he suggests we have a glass of wine and discuss. He's really selling it too—"Come on, Kate, we'll turn off the lights so all we have is the candlelight, I'm sure your feet are sore from wearing heels last night and from the hike today and could use a good massage. I promise it will feel amazing…"

183

While he's talking I'm thinking about his hands all over me and my resistance is waning. "You're wearing me down, you know." While we drink our wine, he's rubbing the top of my hand and when he starts kissing my fingers, that's it. I want him touching me everywhere, so I agree to the massage.

He turns off the lights, brings the candle over to the night table, and turns the bed down. I go into the bathroom and take off everything except for my bra and underwear, and now I'm grateful that I chose to bring my prettiest lacy sets with me. I slip on the fluffy hotel robe and slippers, and I'm suddenly very nervous. We've touched each other plenty, but he's never seen me in just my bra and underwear. It takes me a minute to get up the courage to finally leave the bathroom.

When I come out, he's sitting on the bed waiting for me. He has some spa-like music playing on his phone and tells me to come over and lie down. I admit to him that I'm really nervous.

"Kate, I would never push you to do anything you don't want to do, so we don't have to do this, okay? But if you're nervous just because of me seeing you undressed, then don't be. I think you look incredible, and I just want to make you feel good and do something for you. And we can stop if you feel uncomfortable."

"No, I want to. I'm just shy."

"I understand. I'll turn around and you can get under the sheet, okay?" I'm so happy he suggested that and I agree. After I'm under the sheet, he asks me to roll over onto my stomach. He opens the cap on the bottle of oil, and it smells great, exactly how the kitchen smells when cinnamon rolls are baking. That mixed with the smell of blueberry pie makes me feel like I'm in the middle of a bakery.

Before I can say anything he says, "Oh wow, I might try to drink this." And then we both laugh. He tells me that he wants me to keep my eyes closed the entire time he's massaging me, and I mutter my agreement. Then he lowers the sheet down to my waist. I feel his warm, slippery hands massaging the back of my arms and my shoulders. It already feels amazing and I want more.

He whispers, "Kate, is it all right if I unhook your bra? I don't need you to take it off. I just want to be able to massage your back without getting oil all over it."

"Sure, go ahead," my voice cracks. I feel my bra being unhooked, and then his hands are sliding up and down my back with just the right amount of pressure. I'm already more relaxed than I dreamed I would be, and after he spends at least ten minutes on my back, I feel the sheet being pulled down my legs until I'm completely uncovered. He starts to hook my bra, and I say, "No, it's fine, just leave it."

The next thing I feel are his hands on my thighs, then my calves, and then my feet. I can't stop telling him how amazing it feels, and he just keeps telling me to just relax and enjoy it. After what seems like a very long time, he asks me to roll over on my back but to remember to keep my eyes closed. When I roll over, my bra is flopping loosely. It's really going to be in the way, so I grit my teeth and take it off, my eyes still shut.

I hear Jordan inhale sharply and he whispers, "Are you sure, Kate? You don't have to."

I just nod and say, "Mmm, hmm."

"So beautiful," he whispers and then proceeds to massage my arms and across my chest, avoiding my breasts. He runs his oiled fingers lightly across my stomach, and I'm completely relaxed. Then he massages the front of my thighs and calves and gives my feet another round of rubbing.

Every muscle in my body is relaxed, and I think that it's over—he's done my entire body, front and back. I open my eyes, but he tells me to close them again. I feel his fingers back on my thighs, but with a much lighter touch this time. I smile and say, "Oh, I get it, you want to torture me a little."

He says, "Something like that." He continues stroking my thighs lightly making his way closer and closer to my panties. Then he softly drags his fingers up and down the super sensitive area at the top of my inner thighs.

I'm shaking and my back arches off the bed. "I won't be able to stand much more of that," I say.

He says, "Shh, just enjoy it. Just enjoy it." It feels incredible, and I'm suddenly aware of how heavy I'm breathing now. He snaps me out of my euphoria when he whispers, "Kate, I want to do something for you. You can stop me if you are uncomfortable, or you can say no, okay?"

I don't know what he has in mind, but I just keep my eyes closed and whisper, "Okay." Then I feel my panties slowly being pulled down. I immediately tense up, and he says, "We don't have to do this. Just tell me to stop, Kate."

Part of me knows we should stop, but another part, a much bigger part, wants him to keep going. I manage to whisper, "Keep going." He takes my panties off, and I gasp when I feel the feather light touch of his fingers on me. He's softly stroking me over and over. I feel like it's suddenly a hundred degrees in the room, and all I can say is, "That feels so good."

He says, "Just the beginning beautiful. Now don't move. Just let me make you feel good." He spends the next few minutes kissing me where I haven't been kissed in such a long time.

I can't possibly stay still with what he's doing to me. This goes on for what seems like forever, and now I'm begging, "Please, Jordan, more!" With that he increases the speed and pressure, and I feel myself about to let go. But just before I do, he slows down again.

He repeats this process over and over again, and just when I'm certain that I can't possibly take another second, he finally says, "Let go, Kate" and pushes me over the edge. I almost feel like I lost consciousness for a second because the next thing I know, he's lying down beside me.

I finally open my eyes, and he's looking at me and smiling from ear to ear. He strokes my cheek and says, "That was incredible Kate. I want to do it again and again." I blush and say that I would have a hard time saying no to that. He looks down at my body, and at that moment, I realize that I'm completely exposed. I quickly grab the sheet and pull it up to my chest.

His smile disappears and he says, "I can see your scars." I look down, thinking that part of my stomach must still be uncovered. I've got several scars from my childhood surgeries and some stretch marks from being overweight. I try to pull the sheet tighter but he gently grabs my wrist and says, "No, I'm not talking about your body, I see your heart scars, Kate. They were put there by all those people from your past who have driven into your head that you are unattractive and unworthy. Sure, you can get past those terrible things and your heart heals in time, but it always leaves a little scar. And unfortunately, you've got a lot of them."

I just nod and, again, wonder where in the hell this guy came from. I've never heard all my insecurities described so well. And just like that, I know that I can trust him not to hurt me. I pull the sheet down and point out every real scar I have, tell him which surgeries go with each scar, and he thanks me for telling him.

We lay there quietly for a few minutes before I finally spit it out. "Jordan, I want nothing more than to make you feel as good as you just made me feel."

"I really want that too. You have no idea how hard it is for me to say no, but I want this weekend to just be about you." Before I can protest, he says, "I will definitely take a rain check though."

I smile and say, "You got it." He says, "And before I'm tempted to change my mind, I'm going back to my room. I think we will both sleep very well tonight. Check out is at eleven, so I'll be back at about 10:45 tomorrow." And again, before I can protest, he gives me a quick kiss, puts on his shoes, tells me goodnight, and walks out the door.

I sleep until after eight the next morning, and as soon as I wake up, I immediately start thinking about the night before. The room still smells like blueberries and cinnamon, and I can't stop smiling. Then I realize I'm really hungry. We never ate anything after brunch yesterday. I get up, brush my teeth, and shower. After I've put on my makeup and dried my hair, I pack up my stuff and wait for Jordan. I check my phone, and I have a text from the pet sitter with a picture of Max at the dog park this morning. I also have a text from Noah that came in at eleven thirty last night:

***Glad you are having a good time. I've been really busy and visited six clinics yesterday. I'm ready to come home. My flight gets in at 6:45 tomorrow and I'm going to get a ride home from the airport. See you around 8 tomorrow night. Love you.***

Now my happy feelings are replaced with that now-familiar, sickening feeling of guilt. I know something has to give here soon, but I can't make myself think about it right now.

Jordan is knocking on my door at 10:20. When I open it, he says, "Sorry, I know I'm a little early, but I woke up so hungry and figured that you probably are too. Do you want to go ahead and check out and get something to eat?" I tell him that sounds great because I'm starving.

We find a breakfast place just up the street and share an omelet and a stack of pancakes. We both want to go back to the candle shop, so we stop there before we leave to drive home. I buy two more candles; one called apple pie and another one called lemon scones. I also buy a bottle of the same massage oil that Jordan used on me last night and a wine bottle stopper in the shape of a hot air balloon. Jordan buys the blueberry pie candle and another bottle of massage oil; this time he picks out one called warm blueberry pancakes. He asks me to smell it, and it's just as amazing as the one from last night. It's a lot like the candle but also smells like maple syrup.

"Ooh, that smells really good," I say.

He smiles and says, "Yeah, it will smell even better on you."

I blush and playfully slap his arm, whispering, "Jordan!"

We drive home and, again, it feels like it only takes minutes to get there. We talk and laugh the whole way and time flies. When we get to his house, I'm not happy about the fact that I have to leave right away. I need to get home, unpack, and get everything put away before Noah gets back. Jordan puts my bag in my trunk for me and pulls me in for a hug and a long, slow kiss. I tell him that I can't thank him enough for the best weekend I've ever had, that he went way overboard for me, and that I can't wait until next weekend. Then it will my turn to spoil him. He tells me that he had the most amazing time too, and he'll be counting the hours until Friday.

When I leave, I feel it. I actually feel a physical ache inside me. Jordan has become very important to me, and again, I know that we can't go on like this forever. I try to push those thoughts away by replaying every detail of the weekend, and by the time I pull in my own driveway, I'm smiling again.

When I get in the house, I unpack my bag, put it away in the closet, and start a load of laundry. It's a little past five, and I see that I have a text from Liz. She tells me that Tara's school took first place at the competition for the second year in a row. I text her back and tell her to congratulate Tara for me and that she can count on me to be there next year. The pet sitter walked Max at about three thirty, so I don't have to take him out. He's following me around, so I play with him for a little while.

I'm sitting on the couch reading when Noah walks in a few minutes before eight.

He says, "Hi. How are you?"

"Hi. I'm fine. How was your trip?"

He simply says, "It was fine." I'm used to a twenty-minute story about every detail, so I know he's taking my comments about talking about work too much to the extreme.

I just say, "That's good."

He stands there for a few seconds and then says, "I'm going to take a shower. Do we have any frozen pizza?" I nod. "Can you put one in the oven for me, please?"

I put my book down and say, "Sure, no problem."

He drops his bag in the office, and I preheat the oven for his cauliflower crust mushroom pizza.

After he showers I sit at the table with him while he eats. I say, "So, tell me about the trip. How was your hotel?"

"Good," he responds. I ask him a few more questions, and every one of them is met with a one-word response, so I stop trying. Point taken, Noah. I tell him that I'm going to go to bed, and he says he'll be in a bit after he checks his email. I'm asleep by the time he finally comes to bed.

***

The following week is the typical routine. Work, then dinner at home with Noah and watching TV at night. One difference this week is that Jordan and I are texting back and forth every day, sometimes several times a day. And every time I get a message from him, I'm excited and happy.

Noah is going back to Tennessee this weekend and tells me he has the same flight out on Thursday morning that he had last week, but this time his flight home gets in at 4:15 on Sunday. He asks me if I can pick him up then, and I tell him I'll be there.

When he leaves on Thursday, he gives me a quick kiss, tells me to have a great weekend, and says he loves me. I tell him I love him too, but I'm relieved when he walks out the door. I'm mostly relieved because looking at Noah is causing me to feel sick with guilt. I never dreamed that I'd be doing what I'm doing. How can I keep this up? Noah is my husband, and we made promises to each other when we got married. But I can't stay away from Jordan. He has made me feel beautiful and seen again, and I don't want those feelings to stop.

I take a deep breath and pull myself together before the tears start, and then I head out the door to go to work.

# CHAPTER 33
# 2023

After what seems like weeks, Friday is finally here. Jordan texted me yesterday:

*Did you see that it's supposed to be rainy and stormy most of the weekend? Temperature is supposed to drop too. I'm thinking comfy clothes, blanket, and wine in front of the fireplace. How does that sound? If that sounds good to you, how about you come over tomorrow afternoon and you can just plan on spending the weekend here? Guest room has clean sheets and is all ready for you.*

I tell him that sounds great. Again, the problem is what to do with Max. But then I reason that Jordan only lives ten minutes from me, so I can just go back home to let him out. As long as he has a last walk no earlier than seven, he's good for the night. I text him back and let him know the plan and that, because of it, I won't be able to come over until about seven thirty tomorrow night. He tells me that's fine and he'll see me then.

I spend Friday in my usual way but feeling giddy excitement all day. I do my workout, run errands, and do laundry. After that I take a long, hot shower and put on my makeup. I put a few waves in my hair and slip on some comfy clothes.

When I take Max out at seven, it's just starting to rain a little and the temperature has dropped at least ten degrees. I set him up with food and water and, even though we don't shut him in his crate at night, I put a pee pad in there and leave the door open just in case he can't wait for me in the morning. I tell him he's a good dog and pat him on the head. Then I throw on a jacket and head to Jordan's.

By the time I pull my car into his garage, it's raining pretty hard and wind is blowing. He opens the door and says, "Hello, gorgeous. I'm so glad you're here." I tell him that I'm so happy to be there, and we hug and kiss for a minute.

He says, "Okay, we are all set up." He's got a fire going and, as promised, and a couple of thick blankets on the floor. There's a bottle of Merlot and two glasses sitting next to the blankets. "We really didn't discuss dinner, so I just picked us up a couple of salads. Hope that's okay." I tell him that sounds perfect, and he tells me to go ahead and sit down. I take my jacket and shoes off and sit down on the blankets.

The fire is toasty warm, and it feels great on this chilly, stormy night. Jordan brings over a little plate of cheese and opens the wine. He asks me how my week was, and we tell each other about the past four days. We only talk about work for a few minutes, and then we turn our conversation to last weekend and how amazing it was. He tells me his favorite part was giving me the massage and what happened afterward. Then he says, "You are really blushing. Why are you embarrassed, Kate?"

"I don't know. I guess, you know, it was really intimate, and it's not easy to be that vulnerable." Then I smile and add, "And you drove me insane, in a good way. I'm a little embarrassed when I think about how, um, crazy turned on you got me."

Now I'm blushing even more, and he says, "You are so damn cute, but you'd better get over it. I really enjoy taking care of you, so much so that it's hard for me to stop, and I plan on making you beg more than once this weekend."

All I can do is say, "Jordan!" And now he's laughing a little. I say, "Okay, that's fine. But I have plans for you too. You just wait and see." Now he's the one blushing, and I feel like I just got some power back.

We sit for about an hour, enjoying the wine and cheese. Then we eat our salads and have a second glass of wine. I've got a little liquid courage going, and I decide to be bold. I say, "So I have an idea. How about we go to your room, you can light that candle you bought, get out the massage oil, and let me give you the massage this time? And I think I know one area that I'm really going to concentrate on. Sound okay?"

"Oh yeah? Someone's feeling naughty."

I'm feeling pretty brave now. "You think so? You haven't seen naughty yet. I have plans for you, Jordan."

He's blushing again and says, "Well, that's an offer I can't turn down."

We go to his room, and he lights the candle that's sitting on his nightstand. He puts on some music, and I say, "Good. Now can you please strip down to your underwear and bring me the massage oil?"

He comes back in a robe and gives me the oil that he used on me last weekend. I tell him I want to use the new oil he bought, but he says, "Nope. I'm saving the maiden voyage of that for you. You'll have to use this one." I don't argue and ask him to please take off his robe and lie down on his stomach.

When he takes off his robe and I see him in his boxer briefs, I finally get to see his body all at once. He obviously takes working out seriously and he's got a well-defined six pack. He's got great biceps, and his thighs are pretty muscular too. "Wow, Jordan, you look great," I say.

He thanks me and says, "Right back at you, beautiful."

I start by rubbing the oil in my hands to warm it up, and then I work on the back of his arms and his back. He's sighing with pleasure with each new spot that I touch. I make my way down the backs of his thighs and his calves but decide to leave his feet until the end. I whisper to him to turn over, and as soon as I start touching his chest and making my way down his stomach, I can clearly see that he's turned on.

I look up and he's watching me. "Nope. Eyes closed. Just like you made me do last weekend. And I want you to keep your hands behind your head."

He smiles and says, "You're the boss." I make my way down his legs and then spend quite a while massaging his feet. He keeps saying, "Feels so good." And I tell him it's about to feel a lot better. I lightly drag my nails from his calves up his thighs and back down again. He groans with pleasure, and I repeat this stroke over and over.

He's breathing hard now. "Kate. I want you so bad." I use the lightest touch of my fingertips to lightly stroke him over his underwear. He's begging for me to touch him harder, and I know he's dying for more.

"Keep your eyes closed and hands behind your head," I say as I slide his underwear off. I return my attention to stroking him, but this time I put a little oil in my hands. I speed up and then slow down over and over again.

It's not long before he says, "I can't take anymore."

"Oh, I think you can," I say, and I keep it up a little longer.

He finally says, "Kate. Please, please, please…" And that's all I needed to hear. It only takes seconds to push him over the edge. He's panting and trying to catch his breath. When he finally does, he says, "You are so bad! You almost killed me, you know."

I get a little nervous that maybe I went too far and say, "Seriously, was it too much?"

He laughs and says, "Yes, but in the very best way possible. I don't think I've ever been that turned on in my life! You are nothing short of incredible, and I loved every second of it!"

I'm elated to hear him say that, and I tell him that he needs to understand that I prefer to give than to receive and he better get used to me wanting to make him feel good. I lie down beside him, and he puts his arms around me.

The next thing I know, I'm waking up to the sound of rain. I open my eyes and see that there's light in the room. The clock says that it's 5:42 a.m. I guess he didn't need to get the guest room ready. This is the first time we've slept in the same bed, and it just feels natural to me. I roll over and watch Jordan sleep. He looks so peaceful, and I don't want to wake him up.

I slide out of bed as quietly as I can, go to the guest bathroom to brush my teeth, and then head out to the kitchen. I make a pot of coffee and see what he has in the fridge for breakfast. He has eggs, turkey sausage, and shredded cheese, so I look through the cabinets for a bowl. When I find a big bowl, I prep an omelet for us.

I put the mixture back in the fridge and find the coffee cups. I pour myself a cup and sit down at the island. While I wait for Jordan to get up, I check my phone and find a message that Noah sent late last night. It's short and just says that he's in his room and has a very busy day ahead of him tomorrow so he's going to bed. I quickly send back an equally short text. I tell him good morning and that I hope he has a good day.

I hear the bedroom door open, and Jordan walks out in just a pair of pajama pants. I think to myself that he looks entirely too sexy for having just gotten out of bed. "Good morning. Did I fall asleep on you? And did you go to the guest room?"

I tell him that we both fell asleep, that I never made it to the guest room, and say that I hope that's okay. He says, "Are you kidding? It's more than okay. I'm just sorry that I slept like a rock and didn't even realize you were sleeping right next to me."

I tell him not to be sorry, and I'm so glad that he slept well. He says, "As if you didn't do enough for me last night, I see you made coffee this morning too." Then he says, "You really surprised me last night. You're usually so shy."

I blush a little at the memory of last night. I shrug and then explain, "I guess my inhibitions start to disappear when I feel attractive and wanted, and that's how you make me feel. So, thank you, Jordan."

He walks over to me and surprises me by putting his arms around me and picking me up. I wrap my legs around his waist, and now our bodies are pressed tightly together. "Kate, I'm so glad that I make you feel that way, but you should always feel sexy and confident, and I hate that sometimes you don't."

I just smile and kiss him. I feel so appreciated and valued at this moment. I'm getting emotional, so I decide to lighten the mood. "Put me down before I end up taking you back in the bedroom," I tell him.

"Promises, promises, Kate." He smiles and gently lowers me to the ground.

I giggle and shake my head. "There's an omelet all mixed up and ready to go in the fridge. I was just waiting for you to get up. How about I go and take the dog out and take a shower, and then I'll come back and make you breakfast?" He tells me that sounds good to him.

It's pouring rain again this morning. We've had a series of storm fronts move through, and it's raining a lot more than it usually does. I take Max out in the front yard. Because of the rain, he doesn't even want to go out but finally gives in. I pet him for a few minutes and give him a fresh water and fill his food bowl.

I wash my makeup off from the night before—I never go to bed without washing my face. It's a big no-no for me, so I must have been really tired last night. After I give my face a good scrubbing, I take another long, hot shower, shave my legs, and wash my hair. When I get out of the shower, I reapply my makeup and blow dry my hair. There's no point in doing anything more with it since it's pouring rain outside. It's chilly so I put on a pair of jeans and a long-sleeve shirt. I tell Max I'll be back to let him out in the afternoon and head out to drive back to Jordan's.

When I get back, it's after nine. Jordan has showered, and, unfortunately, has a shirt on now. I apologize for taking so long. He says it's fine and that he wants me to take all the time

I need because I'm always worth the wait. Then he gets a skillet out and puts it on the stove.

"Hey, hey, hey," I say. "Just stop right there. I said I was going to cook you breakfast." He tries to protest, but I tell him it's not up for discussion.

He smiles and says, "When you decide to do something, you're pretty stubborn, aren't you? I think it's pretty sexy."

I just say, "Good!" and then I cook our omelet and put a couple of English muffins in the toaster. We sit at the table and eat our breakfast, then we drink two more cups of coffee and just talk for most of the morning.

It's a little before noon when Jordan asks me if there's anything I want to do today. I tell him that I've got nothing in mind, and then he's thinking. He says, "Hmm, how about we take a drive? No particular place, but somewhere that's at least an hour away. If it's still raining, we can find a theater and see a movie, or if it's cleared off, we can find a park and go for a walk. Then we can go to a market and pick up a few things for dinner tonight. How does that sound?"

I tell him that sounds good to me. I ask if we can hang out about another half an hour; then I'll go home and let Max out again before we take off for the afternoon. It's a quick trip back home to let the dog out, and then I head back to Jordan's.

We head out with no real destination in mind and drive for about forty-five minutes. We're coming up to a pretty big town and see signs for stores, restaurants, and a movie theater. We pull into the parking lot, intending to go to the theater, but there's a bowling alley right next door, and Jordan asks me if I'd like to do that instead. I tell him to be prepared for the fact that I'm a terrible bowler but that it sounds like fun. It's still pouring rain, and Jordan insists that I let him drop me off at the door.

We take our time and bowl for a couple of hours and, just as I thought, I'm still terrible! Jordan's not much better than I am, but we are just laughing and having a great time. It's after four thirty when we leave and find a market nearby. Once inside we contemplate what we want to eat later. He asks me what I want, and I tell him that I'd like to keep it light, so we agree on shrimp and wild rice. He's got his cooler in the trunk, so we put the shrimp in it and start the drive back home.

Once we get back to his house, it's after six thirty. I tell him I need to let the dog out one last time tonight. He says, "Of course, go ahead and go. I'll get things ready for dinner while you're gone." I tell him I'll be right back and head to my house.

It's not raining anymore, but it's chilly. I walk Max up and down the street and try to stop him from running in all the puddles. When we get home, I have to take him in the bathroom and wipe off his muddy paws. I change into comfy jogger pants and a sweatshirt, down a bottle of water, get Max all set up for the night, and head back over to Jordan's. When I come in, he's got the table set and the indoor grill heating up for the shrimp.

"Welcome back. How about a glass of Pinot Grigio tonight?" I tell him that's an excellent choice and that I would love it. It only takes a few minutes to cook the shrimp, and we are ready to go. He dims the lights and puts some music on and we enjoy our dinner.

We clean up the kitchen together, and he asks me if I'd like to sit in front of the fireplace again tonight. I say, "I sure would. It's chilly outside, and I'm having a hard time staying warm."

He smiles and says, "Well, I think we'll have to work on that then."

I excuse myself, go to the bathroom, and brush my teeth. And he does the same. He gets the fire going, and we sip our wine and talk about what a great weekend it's been. Our glasses are empty, and it's not long before he says, "Let's work on warming you up."

He lays me down on the blankets and we start kissing. He's such a great kisser, and I feel like I could do this for hours. He stops, and when I open my eyes, he's looking at me and smiling.

"What?" I ask.

He says, "I want to ask you a question."

"Sure, ask away."

He clears his throat and says, "Okay, I'm curious. Do you have any fantasies? Like anything that you've always wanted to try but were too shy?"

I wasn't expecting that, and I'm struggling with how to answer him. I say, "Um, sure, I guess everybody does, right? I mean, don't you?"

He looks embarrassed and says, "Yeah, like you said, I'm pretty sure everybody does."

"Well, I'll make you a deal," I say. "You tell me one of yours, and I might tell you one of mine."

He laughs and says, "Oh, I see how you turned that around on me. You want me to go first, huh?"

I tell him that I know it's not fair because he asked me first but, yes, I'd like him to go first. He clears his throat again, pours us what's left of the wine, and leans back on his elbow. He says, "This is tougher than I thought." He pauses for several seconds, takes a big drink of his wine, and then says, "Because I trust you, Kate, here goes—"

I interrupt him. "Before you say anything, I want you to know that I'm not going to judge and that you're right, you can trust me."

He takes a deep breath and starts again, "Okay, here goes. I think it would really turn me on to blindfold you. Please don't misunderstand. I don't mean that I'm into S&M, and I don't even understand that at all. I'd just want to spend a really, really long time touching, kissing, and pleasuring you. I'd tell you that you aren't allowed to touch me at all, and it would be all about you. Knowing that you are at my mercy and forced to just lay back and enjoy every minute of it without being able to see what I'm going to next or be able to reciprocate would make me really happy and would totally turn me on."

I swallow hard and can barely get any words out. I finally manage to say, "Um, wow. I've never done anything like that before, but I think I could get on board with it."

"Really? I'm glad to hear you say that! Okay, now your turn."

"Well, you might or might not be surprised to hear that mine is very similar to yours. Um, like I told you before, I'm a giver. So, I guess I don't know if I'd really call it a fantasy, but I'd like to be able to spend an entire night just taking care of you. And you wouldn't be allowed to give me anything in return. I'd tell you that you're not allowed to move or touch me, and then I'd do exactly what you just said you'd do to me. I would take care of you over and over, and all you would be able to do is just lay there and enjoy it."

We are both smiling from ear to ear, and he says, "Oh, Kate, you have me so turned on right now. Come on." And with that he stands up and extends his hand. I take it and he leads me into his bedroom.

We immediately fall into bed. The room is completely dark, and the only sound is the soft music coming from the speakers in the ceiling. We are kissing and touching each other, and it doesn't take long before we both have all our clothes off. He kisses his way from my neck all the way down to my toes and then all the way back up until he's lying next to me. I feel his hand between my legs and I'm using my hands on him too. He's much more urgent than the last time he had me in this position, and right when I'm about to go over the edge, he stops abruptly.

I'm confused as to why he stopped, and then I feel him stretch out beside me, facing me. He takes my leg over his and hesitates for a moment. I know he's waiting for my okay, so I quickly say, "Yes!" Now he's sliding inside me. He's gentle and takes his time, but before long he's groaning with pleasure. He moves slowly inside me, and I feel his hand on me again. He's using his fingers on me again; making slow, soft circles, and the combination of that and the feeling of him inside me is out of this world. He's moving faster now and we're both so close. I'm losing all control and he's just seconds behind me. We're both panting, and my heart is beating so fast that I can hear it. We finish together.

We don't say anything for at least a full minute after, both catching our breath. "That was incredible!" I finally say.

He laughs and says, "So glad you liked it. You felt amazing. I think I'm addicted to you, Kate." I laugh and then his voice is serious, "I mean it, Kate. I love you."

I'm stunned, and I don't even realize that tears are rolling down my cheeks. I say, "Jordan, I love you too."

He touches my face and feels my tears. Wiping my cheek, he says, "Hey, don't cry. It's okay, it's all going to be okay. How about we go back out and sit in front of the fire and talk?" I nod and we make our way back out to the living room.

We sit down and hold each other. I feel more tears coming, and I turn my head. He says, "Please don't cry, Kate. I can't stand to see you cry."

I wipe my tears and say, "What are we going to do?"

"What do you want to do? Listen, I was married. It was a very happy marriage. I would have *never* cheated on Rachel, and she would never have cheated on me. I don't know what it would be like to be in a less than happy marriage or to be on the receiving end of someone not giving me any affection. I think I would try like hell to make it work, but if I couldn't then I would have to move on."

I nod and say, "Yes, that's exactly what I think too. But to be fair, have I 'tried like hell?' I don't know. I mean, I've tried, but since you came into my life, I'm not really putting in much effort, you know? And as someone who's been cheated on, I know it's not fair to Noah for me to go on like this."

Now I'm crying again, and Jordan has tears in his eyes. He says, "Well, has Noah put in any effort?"

"Not really. And we are fighting more. If anything, we're drifting further and further apart. This sucks! I don't know what to do! Why couldn't I have met you before I met Noah?!"

He says, "Come here, don't cry. You don't know how much I wish that I had met you sooner and that there wasn't another person involved. All I can say is that I love you. I love you so much. And the thought of losing you now hurts so bad that I can't even think about it. But I also know that we can't go on like this forever. I guess I've known that from the beginning, but now it's time we both face it."

I nod in agreement. There's really nothing else to say, and we just hug for long time. He finally says, "Come on, let's go sleep on it." We go back to his bed, where we were so happy just a short time ago, and hold each tight other until we fall asleep.

***

The next morning I awake to Jordan lying beside me, and he's already awake. "Good morning," he says. "I hope you slept okay."

"So-so," I say. "How about you?"

"Same. Let's get up and I'll make us some coffee."

We talk while we have our coffee, and we finally decide that we should both take time and think about what we want to do while we're apart this week.

He says, "I don't mean to put it all on you, Kate, but it's really your decision. I refuse to be the reason you end your marriage. If you decide to end it, you should be doing it because both of you tried to fix it in every way possible and nothing worked. I feel like that's the only way that you will be able to walk away without regret."

As much as I hate what he's saying, I know he's 100 percent correct. I'm crying again and I say, "I guess I'll get going then."

"No, I didn't mean you have to leave right now—"

I interrupt him and say, "I don't want to, but I should. Will I see you next weekend? I mean, can we get together and talk more?"

He looks relieved and says, "Of course we can. I'll see you next weekend for sure."

I force myself out of my chair, grab my purse and jacket, and head out to my car. Before I get in, Jordan grabs me and holds me tight. He strokes my hair and says, "I love you, Kate. I love you. My Kate, my beautiful Kate."

It's more than I can bear to hear, and I'm sobbing when I say, "I love you so much, Jordan." I have to go now, or I'm never going. The last thing I see as I'm leaving his driveway is Jordan with his head down and his face in his hands.

As I'm driving I feel so sick to my stomach that I think I might throw up. I walk Max as fast as I can when I get home, and I then lie down in bed. I feel like the tears are never going to stop. It's one o'clock before I can stop crying and force myself to get up and take a shower. My eyes are swollen and my nose is red. I look like hell. I try to cover it up as best as I can with makeup, but anyone who looks at me can tell I've been crying. I keep seeing Jordan in the garage as I was leaving and the tears keep coming back. I've had to fix my mascara three times already, and I'm wondering how in the world I'm going to be able to go to the airport and pick up Noah today.

I fix my makeup one last time before I leave. The storm front has passed through and it's sunny today, so I'm grateful that I have sunglasses on to hide my swollen eyes. When Noah gets in the car, the first thing he says is, "You okay? I didn't hear much from you at all this weekend." He turns to look at me and says, "Why is your nose all red?"

"I've been sneezing a lot this weekend and don't feel very well. I thought maybe it was just allergies, but now I think I might be getting a cold. Sorry about not calling you. I just didn't feel very well so I slept a lot."

I don't think I sound very convincing, but he says that he's sorry I don't feel well and, for once, I'm grateful when he changes the subject to work and tells me every detail of his trip. When we get home, it's after five and I try my best to keep busy until bedtime. I'm not hungry, but I manage to eat a few bites of the tacos I made for dinner. I pretend to read while Noah watches TV, and we go to bed at nine.

I lean over to give him a kiss goodnight, and he says, "Maybe we shouldn't. You know, if you think you're getting sick." I agree and I turn off the light. Noah is asleep in seconds, but I'm awake most of the night.

# CHAPTER 34
# 2023

I decide not to work out on Monday morning, and I leave for work before Noah gets out of the shower. Work is nothing out of the ordinary all week, but time feels like it's crawling. Jordan and I text each other several times during the week and it's painful. No plans are being made, like we've been doing for the past several weeks, and there's only sadness in our words. We just tell each other "I love you" and talk about how much we miss each other.

Noah leaves for Texas on Thursday morning, and I'm relieved. On Monday I had called my therapist, Nelly Rogers, who I haven't seen since shortly before Noah and I got married, and ask her if I can please see her this week. I ask for two appointments, and she gives me Thursday at four and Friday at one. I ask Anna if she can take my last patient on Thursday, and she tells me she sure can. She knows something's wrong, but I tell her I'm not ready to talk about it yet.

When I get to Nelly's office on Thursday, I'm an emotional wreck. She takes me back to her office and says, "Kate, it's nice to see you. But if you're here and you're already crying, I know something is terribly wrong."

I proceed to talk nonstop for forty minutes. I tell her every detail, from meeting Jordan in the grocery store to how Noah and I have not had intimacy in our marriage for months now. She's been taking notes the whole time I've been talking, and when I finally stop talking, she says, "This has been a lot for you to try to handle on your own. I wish you had called me sooner."

"I know. I should have. I just never dreamed it would get to this point."

"Kate, do you love Noah?"

I'm sobbing but squeak out, "Yes."

Then she says, "Kate, do you love Jordan?"

"I never dreamed that I would, but yes, I'm definitely in love with Jordan."

She takes a moment, then asks, "Kate, did you have sex with Jordan?"

I shrug my shoulders and say, "It depends on what you mean by sex."

She says, "Okay, tell me what *you* mean by that." I go on to tell her all about the time we traveled to Arizona for the weekend and when I spent the weekend at his house. She looks confused, and I try my best to explain.

I tell her, "We kissed and massaged each other, and ended up touching each other very intimately. We described what we wanted to do to each other, going into great detail, but we stopped just short of taking it further."

Nelly looks at me and says, "So when he gave you the massage in the hotel room, there was no sex?"

"He massaged me, just like I said, and he did use his hands on me, but that's where it stopped. He told me how much he would love to do so much more if he could and told me exactly what he would do to me, but we decided we shouldn't go that far."

She nods and says, "Okay, and the time at his house when you gave him the massage?"

"Same thing. I massaged him, and I did use my hands on him too. And the following night we talked about fantasies and got ourselves all worked up. We rolled around in his bed and touched each other intimately again. Afterward, we talked about how much we wanted to do more and, again, described in detail to each other exactly how we would want the experience to go."

Nelly looks at me and asks me, in her best "cut the crap" way, "So, you're being honest with me? You're telling me there was no oral and no intercourse, just using your hands on each other? Am I understanding you correctly?"

I'm crying again and just softly say, "Yes."

She contemplates what she wants to say next and finally says, "Well, it's very difficult to stop yourself in the heat of the moment, and multiple times I might add, so you should at least give yourselves credit for that."

I just shake my head and say, "Yeah, right, big gold star for me. It's still wrong, and I shouldn't have done any of it. I'm married! And I had guys cheat on me so many times in the past! How could I do this?!"

I'm really upset now, and Nelly says, "Kate, listen to me. You can't take 100 percent of the blame. There are two other people involved in this scenario." Then she tells me that we are out of time for today but we will continue tomorrow. She says, "Listen. Until I see you tomorrow, I have two questions for you. I don't want you to answer me now. I want you to think about it tonight and let me know tomorrow. Question one: If you and Noah had still been happily married when Jordan bumped into you in the store that first time, what would you have done? And question two: If you had never met Jordan, would you be contemplating leaving Noah right now or would you want to continue to try to work on your marriage?"

I start to answer, but she interrupts. "No, I don't want a spontaneous answer. I really want you to go home and think about it."

I tell her I will and that I'll see her tomorrow.

When I get home, I have a text from Noah letting me know he landed in Texas. I text back and tell him that I hope he has a good trip. Then I text Jordan:

*Hi. I just want you to know that I miss you so much. Can we get together tomorrow night at your place and talk about things?*

It only takes a few seconds before he responds:

*Of course we can. Why don't you come over at around 6:00? I love you and miss you more.*

I text him back and tell him I'll see him then. I make myself a cup of tea and sit at the kitchen table. I'm not hungry, so I just sit and contemplate the questions that Nelly asked me. And I can't stop my tears because I know what I need to do.

\*\*\*

I go back to Nelly's office the next day, and as soon as I sit down, she says, "So did you think about those two questions, Kate?"

I tell her that I did. "If Noah and I had been happily married, like we were for the first couple of years, I know what would have happened when Jordan bumped into me. Sure, I would have noticed how attractive he is, but I would have just told him not to worry about it and turned my attention back to grocery shopping. I might have told Liz about it the next time I saw her. I probably would have said that this hot guy bumped into me at the store and I thought about jumping into his cart for a minute. We would have laughed about it, but after that I doubt I would have ever thought about him again."

Nelly says, "Okay, now what about the second question?"

I take a deep breath. "I really had to think about this one because now it's hard for me to even picture a time before Jordan was in my life. I know it hasn't been that long, but I feel like I've known him forever." I start to cry again, and she hands me a box of tissues and tells me to continue. I take another deep breath and try to compose myself.

"If I'd never met Jordan I would be fighting like hell for my marriage. I don't want to go through another divorce, and I would try anything and everything to stay married to Noah."

Nelly leans back in her chair and says, "I'm not sure if this is what you want to hear, but the answer to question two tells me that you need to try to give your marriage a chance. Without Jordan in the picture at all. If you don't at least try, I don't think you'll ever be at peace."

I feel like someone has punched me in the stomach, but I finally manage to say, "You're right. I know you're right. But I have no idea how I can say goodbye to him."

"I know it's going to be very difficult, but you won't be able to move on if you don't tell him goodbye."

"I guess I need to tell Noah about Jordan and what's been going on, right?"

I'm surprised when she says, "You know I believe that you have to be completely honest and open and that lying and cheating have no place in a marriage. But I don't think you should tell him."

"Really?" I ask, "How can I not tell him? Isn't that unfair to Noah?"

"Now wait. I didn't say that you're never going to tell him. I just don't want his decisions regarding the problems you two have and whether you should stay together to be clouded by the knowledge that you've been spending time with someone else. I want you to sit him down and have a serious discussion about the problems in your marriage. Tell him how unhappy you've been and ask him if he wants to continue with the marriage. If he does, then I want you two to start seeing me at least twice a week. And one of the first things we'll do at that point is have you tell him about Jordan, but while you're here in my office. That way I can guide you both through what to do next. Sound good?"

I tell her that I agree and would rather do it that way because I'd like to have her there to mediate our conversation after I tell Noah.

"Now, here's the hardest part of all. You have to tell Jordan that, for now at least, you are recommitting to your marriage. And that means no more contact at all, including calls and texts. I know how hard this is going to be for you, Kate, but you need to focus all your energy and attention on your marriage. Then, if you exhaust all options or Noah doesn't want to move forward, you can decide what's best for you. And even at that point, I wouldn't recommend jumping right into a relationship with Jordan. I would highly recommend that you spend some time alone, figuring out if you really want to be with him or he just came along at the right time when you needed someone."

I hate what she's saying, and I hate even more that I know she's right. I just nod in agreement, and she says, "Okay, I want to see you and Noah next week. How about Monday at nine?"

I tell her that Noah has one more weekend that he has to travel for work and ask if we can make it for a week from Monday. I don't want to start this and then have him gone for four days again. She agrees and we push it out a week. She tells me that she'll see Noah and me a week from Monday, and I leave the office having no idea how I'm going to do what I have to do tonight. But I know that I have to do it.

When I get home, I try to pull myself together, but I can't. I try to lie down for a nap, but I can't sleep. I just keep playing everything over and over in my head, and I can't believe that anyone can cry as much as I'm crying.

At 5:15 I take Max out for a quick walk and then leave to go to Jordan's. All I can think is how in the hell am I going to do this?! When I pull into his garage, he comes right out and hugs me like he's always done.

He looks at me and says, "Oh, Kate. You look like you've been crying for days. Oh, baby, I'm so sorry, so very sorry."

I just shake my head and tell him he's got nothing to be sorry about. We go in and sit on the couch together. He tells me that he's missed me so much, and I tell him that I've missed him more. Then I say, "I just have to say this right now. Because if I don't, I know I won't be able to."

He looks down and nods as I start talking, "Jordan. There is no doubt in my mind that I love you. You have made the past couple months of my life so wonderful. You are the most amazing man. You are so giving, smart, funny, sexy, kind, loving...I could go on and on. I don't even want to say what I have to say."

I'm crying again and he hugs me and says, "Don't cry, please. Go ahead, go ahead."

I take a deep breath. "I need to try to give my marriage a shot. I have no idea if it will work or not, but if I'd never met you, I know that I would be fighting for my marriage. And I also know that if the marriage had been good, I would have never gone for coffee with you that very first time. It's the only way to be fair to myself, to you, and to Noah. And if it doesn't work out, then I need to spend a little time alone to get my shit together before I can ever be a good partner to you."

He has tears running down his cheeks now and wipes them with the back of his hand. He nods and says, "Everything you just said is completely logical and makes sense, but I'm going to be selfish for a second, okay? I'm being selfish because in this moment, I should just let you leave and not make it any harder on you, but I can't let you go without telling you a few things."

I just nod. "I love you, Kate. I have absolutely no doubt that I am 100 percent, over the top, crazy in love with you. I never felt that way before Rachel and haven't felt that way since I lost Rachel until you came into my life. I know now that's why I felt the need to talk to you in the grocery store that day and why I wanted to continue to see you, even though I knew it was wrong. You are such an amazing woman, and I can't possibly list every wonderful thing about you. I'll just say that if you were my wife, there would never be one day of your life that you would ever have to question if I loved you or if I was attracted to you. And I mean that. As much as I want to beg you not to go, and, believe me, it's taking everything I have not to, I have to respect your decision. So…"

Now he's really crying, and I'm sobbing so hard I can barely catch my breath. He's finally able to talk again and continues, "So I'm going to let you go, and I won't contact you in any way. I want you to take your time and figure out what you need. And I'm going to try to just go on with my life and hope that someday you will be back in it again."

I know that if I don't walk away right now, I never will. I hug him as hard as I can, and I swear the hug lasts a full five minutes. I tell him I love him one last time, manage to stand up and walk to the door, and he doesn't follow. I take one last look back, and he's looking the other way. I can see that he's crying just as hard as I am.

I get in my car and just drive. I drive around for over two hours, crying and wondering to myself if I'm doing the right thing. I fight the urge to drive straight back to Jordan's at least a half a dozen times.

When I get home, I try to call Noah, but he doesn't answer. I text him and tell him that I'm going to bed. I do go to bed, but sleep is not in the cards for me tonight. I toss and turn most of the night until I finally get out of bed at four thirty and make a pot of coffee. As I check my phone, I think to myself that if Jordan has texted me, asking me to please come back to him, I would be in my car in a heartbeat. I glance down. No messages.

I spend the day on the couch drifting in and out of sleep, crying and thinking so hard that my head hurts. But I have to try to think about my marriage. Noah doesn't deserve me leaving without giving him a chance to try to repair it with me. I think back to when we first got together and how good it was, and I can't just throw it away. We were so in love, had so much fun together and couldn't get enough of each other. We used to talk for hours and never ran out of things to say. We were so attracted to each other that we spent a lot of our time in bed. He was so attentive, sweet and romantic. It wasn't that long ago that I couldn't imagine my life without him. I just wish I knew what's changed in the past year and how we've ended up where we are.

# CHAPTER 35
# 2023

On Sunday I pick Noah up at the airport in the late afternoon. The first thing he tells me is that he has to go back to Texas next weekend, but it's going to be a shorter trip, just Thursday and Friday, and he will be back in the late afternoon on Saturday instead of Sunday.

We make small talk on the drive home, but as soon as we get in the house I say, "Noah, let's sit at the dining room table. We need to talk about some stuff."

He takes his suitcase into the office and joins me at the table. Max is trying to jump on him, so I put him in his crate. Noah starts to protest, but I say, "No. No interruptions. He'll be fine."

He looks irritated and says, "I don't know why he can't be out here. I haven't seen him since Thursday…"

"Noah, please, just for a little while."

"Well, what do you want to talk about?"

"Noah, I'm not happy. I haven't been happy for quite some time. And I don't think you're happy either. I feel like we've really become distant, and most of the time I feel like we're just roommates. I miss what we had. I'm lonely and frustrated, and I don't feel like you're attracted to me at all anymore—"

"Are you saying you want a divorce?" he interrupts.

"No. That's what I'm trying to tell you. I still love you, and I want to try to work on things. I want us to go get some counseling and see if we can fix this. If you want to. Do you want to?"

He doesn't really look very concerned and says, "I don't really think that's necessary, but I guess I'll go if I have to."

It's all I can do not to start yelling. What the hell kind of answer is that?! I say, "Try to control your enthusiasm, Noah!"

"Sorry, I just didn't expect this. I don't think anything's wrong. I've just been really busy, and I don't think you understand how hard I'm having to work." I'm even more irritated, but I try to keep my composure.

I take a breath and say, "I know how hard you're working, Noah. But I work hard too. Having less time together shouldn't destroy our marriage. If it does then I don't feel like it was as strong as we thought it was."

He just sighs and says, "When do you want to go?" I tell him that we have an appointment a week from tomorrow at nine, and he says, "Are we done for now? I want to take and shower and let Max out of his crate."

I have so much more that I want to talk about, but I just say, "Sure. We can be done for now." After he showers, he plays with Max and then we watch TV in silence until bedtime.

***

I can't remember a week that has taken so long to get over. Every day feels like it's a month long. I'm not sleeping well, and I'm having difficulty concentrating on anything.

Everyone at work, especially Anna and Dr. Taylor, knows that something's wrong. They have both pulled me aside and asked me what's wrong and if they can do anything for me. I tell both of them that I'll be fine, I appreciate their concern, but I'm not ready to talk about it yet. Neither one of them pushes and I'm grateful.

Jordan has kept his promise, and I haven't heard a word from him since our painful goodbye. I'm relieved when Noah leaves on Thursday and I spend most of Friday and Saturday lying on the couch. I'm either napping or crying, and I can't imagine how this is going to get any better.

Noah's plane is due to land at 5:10 on Saturday, so a few hours before that, I take a shower and try to make myself presentable. Nothing is helping my swollen eyes, but I do the best I can before I leave to pick him up. Even though I don't feel much like eating I've planned a nice dinner for us and I'm going to try to enjoy the evening with him. I need to take a first step in trying to fix this, so I'm going to try to be as positive as I can.

When we get home, he does his usual routine of dropping his bag in the office and playing with Max. I tell him that I've got dinner made and I just need to warm it up in the oven. I dim the lights and put on some music. We sit down to eat, and things feel awkward, but I'm determined to try. I try to reminisce about trips we took when we first got together and how much fun we had when we first got married. He agrees but doesn't add much to the conversation.

He brings up work, and I tell him that I'd like to not talk about work and just concentrate on us. He says, "Sure, whatever," but then becomes silent. I reason with myself that this is going to take time, and we definitely need Nelly to guide us through how to talk to each other again.

After dinner he says, "It looks like it might rain again, so I'm going to go ahead and walk Max before it starts."

When he leaves I decide to unpack his bag for him. I tell myself that it's just another way for me to make an effort and he will probably appreciate it. I unpack his clothes and make two piles, one for the washing machine and one for the dry cleaner's.

After the bag is unpacked, I pick it up to put it in the closet, but I hear something slide inside it. I must have missed something. A belt? I unzip it again, but I don't see anything.

Then I unzip the lining and I find a card. The envelope simply says "K."

I instantly feel like a total asshole because he obviously bought me a card, which is completely out of character for him. He's always said that cards are a waste of money and I've rarely gotten one, even on my birthday. Then I'm thinking, what could the card be for? It's not our anniversary or my birthday.

I turn it over and see that the flap is tucked in but it's not sealed. I debate if I should open it or not and decide to put it back and wait for him to give it to me. I start to zip the lining back up, but curiosity gets the best of me, and I open the envelope.

The card has some sort of poem on the front about love. I read it quickly, and my eyes fill with tears. Have I just been overreacting this whole time? Maybe Noah really has just been tired and overworked, and I blew everything out of proportion. How could I be so stupid?! I jeopardized my marriage and fell in love with another man! I read the front of the card again and feel like I'm going to throw up. I need to apologize to Noah. He really does love me, and I've probably ruined everything! My hands are shaking so much I can barely make my fingers work. I finally get the card open, and there's a handwritten message inside:

*My Dearest Kristen,*

*These past few months have been the best of my entire life. I've had so much fun with you. I can't stop thinking about all of our romantic dinners together and, especially, making love to you over and over again! It's so painful when we have to say goodbye, and I'm counting the minutes until we can be together again. I can't wait until I see you again, you beautiful, sexy, amazing woman!*

*Love you to the moon and back,*
*Noah*

What. The. Fuck?! I read it ten more times until it sinks in. Who in the hell is Kristen?!

My feeling of guilt is gone, just like that, and now all I feel is anger. My first thought is that I can't wait until Noah walks through that front door so I can throw the card in his face and ask him what in the hell is going on. But then I decide not to. I want to try to find out who this Kristen is. I put the card in a drawer in the kitchen and put the suitcase away. I try to pull myself together, but my head is spinning.

By the time Noah comes back, it's raining and he and Max are wet. He says he's going to put Max in the tub to wash his muddy paws and then he's going to take a shower. I try to sound normal and say, "Sure. I'm think I'm going to make some coffee."

As soon as I hear the shower running, I get his phone and punch in his code. But the phone doesn't unlock. I try again, but it's still locked. He's changed his code. I think about what it could be and try Max's birthday. Bingo! It unlocks.

I quickly scroll through his contacts and find a Kristen. She works in human resources at his company's Sacramento office. There's a lot of messages between them and some pictures of her in lingerie. I want to read them all, but I know I don't have much time. What I want to know most of all is when it all started. As far as I can tell, it started about ten months ago.

I also find a contact listed just as "S." There's only a few messages. From what I can determine, she's a bartender at the hotel in Florida that Noah stayed at a few weeks ago. According to the messages, she and Noah had a one-night stand.

I feel sick to my stomach, but I keep looking. There's also a contact listed as just "P." There are tons of messages, dating back to even before Noah and I got married, and a bunch of pictures. As soon as I see her face, I know who she is. Her name is Paige, and she is the last girl Noah dated before we met. I found a picture of her in his desk once, and he had told me that he forgot that he had it and threw it away. Some of the pictures on his phone are of her in a bikini on a beach, and some are of her in her bra and underwear. There is a lot of flirtatious banter, and I want to read more but I hear the shower shut off. I put the phone on the counter and get the card out of the drawer.

When Noah comes out of the bedroom, I'm standing in the kitchen with the card behind my back. He looks at me puzzled and says, "Hey, did you make coffee or do you want to have a glass of wine or something?" He notices that I'm not moving. "What's wrong?"

"Oh, nothing. I unpacked your bag for you." He looks surprised and hesitantly says, "Thanks." Then I pull the card out from behind my back. "It was so sweet of you to get me a card. No, wait, it's for Kristen! The woman that you've been fucking for almost a year!"

All the color drains out of his face, and all he can manage to say is "Shit."

I'm yelling now, "Yep. *Shit* is right, Noah. How many are there, huh? How many?! I also know about the bartender and about Paige. You should have known better than to use Max's birthday as your code. It didn't take much for me to guess it."

I throw the card at him and he says, "Kate, wait. I'm sorry. I don't know what to say."

"Well, you'd better come up with something."

"Okay, okay, when we got married, I was sure it was what I wanted, and I did love you, Kate, and I still do. But I just didn't realize how much I would miss being single. It just started as flirting with Kristen, but then it became more. She works in the office in Sacramento sometimes, but she mainly works remote, so that's how she's been able to meet up with me when I've traveled these past few months."

I'm screaming inside, but I just stay silent and think to myself, keep going, Noah, because now you're telling me things I didn't even know!

"And the bartender was just a one-night thing. I was in the bar having a drink before I went to my room for the night, and she started coming on to me. She was hot, and I was lonely, and it just happened. And as far as Paige goes, we just have this chemistry between us and can't seem to let each other go—"

"Stop. Just stop, Noah! You're pathetic. So, you mean to tell me that all these months that you haven't touched me, and I've beat myself up over and over again and felt unattractive and unloved, that this has been going on?! So those couple of times when you came home from a trip and you wanted to take me out to dinner or cuddle up to me at night it was because you felt guilty for fucking someone else?!"

He doesn't say anything and just shrugs his shoulders. All I can do is scream, "You son of a bitch!"

"I'm so sorry, Kate. I just think that maybe I'm the type of guy that needs to be with more than one woman. Or I might just need to be single for a while and spread my wings a bit, I don't know. I just don't know what I want."

I laugh and say, "Oh, please! You're a little young for the midlife crisis thing, aren't you?" And before he can say anything else, I say, "Get your shit and get the fuck out." He doesn't protest. He packs a bag and leaves, taking Max with him.

As soon as the door shuts, I sink down to the floor and just sit there. Stunned. What in the hell just happened?! I never dreamed that all this had been going on, never even suspected it. I thought about the past few months and how he was "getting ice" at ten o'clock at night once when I called him, and I remember hearing him in the bar once. Was he ever with her when I texted or called? I'm sick just thinking about it. I don't shed another tear—I think it's because I'm too shocked to feel anything except for disbelief and anger right now. I sit on the floor for almost an hour, and by the time I stand up I can't do anything but go to bed.

*** 

The next morning I wake up wondering if I dreamed last night. But Noah isn't beside me, and I know it's not a dream. I get up and make coffee. While I'm sitting at the dining room table, I'm thinking that I want to hurt Noah as much as he's hurt me. I want to tell him that I've been spending time with a real man and I'm glad he wants to "spread his wings" because I'm more than happy to let him go.

But I decide that I won't do that. I don't want him to have any excuses to feel better about what he did. I know that seeing Jordan was wrong, but I ended it and wanted to try to fix my marriage. I just wish I had found out a long time ago because I would have had no problem kicking Noah to the curb.

I think about calling Jordan, but I remember what Nelly said and force myself not to. I'm so confused right now and I need time to pull myself together.

As I'm sitting at the table contemplating what in the hell I'm going to do, Noah walks through the door. As soon as I see his face, I suddenly know exactly what I need to do.

He starts to say, "Kate, I—"

I cut him off immediately and say, "Nope, here's how this is going to go. You are leaving, and I'm going to find another place to live. Once I do I'm taking half of what's in our bank account and anything else I want. I'm filing for divorce. There is nothing else to discuss."

He just nods and says, "I just want you to know that I'm staying at the Hilton and not with a woman. And I'm so sorry, Kate. I did a lot of thinking last night, and I don't know, maybe there's a chance we can work this out. I'm just really confused right now."

I just look away and say, "Please. Just go pack what you need and leave. There's no way I could ever trust you again. You travel all the time for your job, and I would always be wondering if you're with someone. Unless you're willing to find a different job." I say that to see if he's even the slightest bit interested in trying to keep me.

I get my answer when he says, "I can't do that, Kate. I've worked too hard to get where I am. Try to understand."

"Oh, I do understand. You've made everything crystal clear."

When he's ready to go, he says, "I'm leaving now. Again, I'm sorry. Do you want to say goodbye to Max?"

And this is the first time I shed a tear since this nightmare started last night. I pet Max, kiss his head, and tell him that even though he's a pain in the ass, I love him and I will miss him.

Noah tries one last time and says, "I know you're really upset right now, but can I call you? Maybe later this week?"

A part of me wants to say yes. It takes everything in me to say, "No. We're done Noah. Just go." He nods and I see tears in his eyes as he walks out the door.

# CHAPTER 36
# 2023

I take a personal day on Monday and show up for what was supposed to be our marriage counseling session alone. As soon as Nelly takes me back to her office, she says, "What happened? Did Noah refuse to come?"

"I'll try to give you the short version…" I tell her what happened on Saturday night.

When I'm done she actually looks shocked and says, "Geez, Kate, he's an asshole!" I smile for the first time in days. This is why I love her—she's a total professional but also knows when to stop being my therapist and just say it like it is with no bullshit. "Sorry, that wasn't professional. Now I'm going to put my counselor hat back on and ask you if you want to try to salvage the marriage and if you'd like me to help you do that. Affairs don't always mean that the marriage is over, and it is possible to come back from it and be happily married again. I've helped lots of couple rebuild trust and go on to have a successful marriage after infidelity."

"Absolutely not. I told him I'm filing for divorce. My problem now is that I'm so overwhelmed with about a million different thoughts and emotions that I can barely function."

She asks me if I broke down and called Jordan, and I tell her that although I almost did about a thousand times, I didn't.

She's happy to hear that and says, "Okay, here's the plan. You're going to concentrate on you. No texting or calling Jordan because it will only confuse you. If you're 100 percent sure you want to get a divorce, then get yourself a new place to live ASAP, get the divorce papers drawn up, and I want to see you once a week without fail. Got it?"

I tell her that I promise and make a standing appointment every Friday for the next three months.

After my appointment I stop by my office. The girls at the desk say, "What are you doing here? Aren't you off today?"

I tell them yes, but I need to talk to Dr. Taylor. He's with a patient, so I wait in the back hallway for him to get done. Anna is walking a patient out, and when she sees me, she mouths, "What's going on?" and I mouth back, "Later."

When Dr. Taylor is free, he takes me in his office, and as soon as the door closes, he says, "I know something's been bothering you. You're not leaving me are you, Kate? I value you so much, and I don't want to lose you."

"No, nothing like that. But there is some stuff going on that I just can't talk about right now. I need to ask a favor. I need to take the next two weeks off to get some things straightened out. I have PTO, and if you need me to…"

Before I can finish, he puts his hand up, picks up his phone, and rings the front desk. When one of the girls answers, he says, "Hi, Linda. Can you please call the temp agency and tell them that I'm going to need a hygienist for the rest of this week and all of next week? Thanks."

Then he says, "I'll get a temp in here, Kate. I can help Anna if we fall behind and you take as much time as you need."

I'm tearing up and whisper, "Thanks, doc."

"You don't have to thank me. Now do what you need to do and take care of yourself. Let me know if there's anything else I can do."

I nod and slip out the back door when I leave. Later that night I call Anna and tell her the whole story. She is shocked, and the first thing she asks is how she can help. I thank her and tell her that I'll let her know. Then her usual sarcastic sense of humor is on full display. She rattles off a series of insults for Noah, and by the time I hang up, I'm actually laughing.

The next task is to tell Liz. I text her and ask if we can meet for dinner tomorrow night because I have something important to tell her. She responds "absolutely" immediately, and we plan to meet up at six the next night.

As soon as she sees me, she says, "What's wrong? You look like you haven't slept in days." I tell her that she's pretty much right, and for the third time in two days, I rattle off the entire story. She's silent for most of it except for the occasional "What?" or "You've got to be kidding?"

I feel bad when her final question is, "What I can't understand is why you didn't tell me any of this before."

"I know. I'm sorry. It was partially because I felt bad about seeing Jordan, and I felt really embarrassed that my third marriage was in trouble. I really wanted to talk to you, but I just didn't know what to say."

She's serious, which is rare for either one of us when we're together, and says, "Kate. I would never put you down our judge you. I'm not perfect, and my marriage isn't always a bed of roses either, so I'd have a lot of nerve and I'd be a terrible friend if I judged you."

I'm crying now and I say, "I know. I should have told you. I'm sorry."

She says, "It's okay. Don't cry." She pauses and then says, "And as far as Noah is concerned, why doesn't he spread his wings and fly up his own ass?!" That puts an immediate end to my tears, and we're both laughing hysterically.

***

The next couple of weeks are a blur. I find a nice condo to rent not too far from where I'm living now and file for divorce. Noah tries to communicate with me, almost daily, but I keep our conversations strictly about the divorce and dividing our assets. He feels guilty, and because I let him keep the house, he gives me a lump sum of money, which he had to draw out of his retirement account, to compensate for what would have been my half if we had sold it. My lawyer wanted me to go for the house, but I honestly didn't want it—too many bad memories. But she's happy with the fact that I get half of what it's worth.

I decide not to take any of the furniture except for the bed in the guest room and a television. I also take some dishes, but that's about it. I force myself to go out and shop for new furniture and all the other things it takes to furnish my new place. I check my bank account at the end of the two weeks and see that Dr. Taylor didn't make me use any of my PTO and still paid me my full salary for the time I was off. He's the best.

After the dust settles and I'm back to work, I sink into what I can only describe as a deep depression. I'm sad and lonely, and I'm just not finding joy in much of anything anymore. Sure, I have fun with Liz and Anna when we get together, but as soon as I'm alone again, I can't stop thinking about everything that has happened.

I hurt. Bad. My days are all about work, and nights are reading or watching TV. I've stuck to my promise to Nelly: I haven't texted or called Jordan, and he hasn't reached out to me either. I spend a lot of time wondering if he misses me as much as I miss him.

# CHAPTER 37
# 2024

It's been almost six months since I left Noah. I wake up one Saturday morning and take a good, long look in the mirror. I don't like what I see. I've lost fifteen pounds, and my cheeks look hollow. I stopped working out when I moved into my condo. It's been all I can do to function day to day, and the last thing on my mind was fitness. My stomach looks sunken in, I have terrible dark circles under my eyes, and I haven't been to the salon to have my hair colored in months. I have a lot of dark roots and gray hairs showing, and I suddenly realize how bad it looks.

I look at myself and say, "Enough, Kate. It's time to start living again." I put on one of my old workout DVDs and try to get through it. I only make it halfway through before I'm struggling to catch my breath and have a cramp in my side, but I'm proud of myself for making it that far. After that I take a long shower, scrub my hair and my face, and apply a thick layer of moisturizer on my skin when I get out.

After I get dressed, I call my salon and make an appointment to get my roots done and ask my stylist to give me lots of blonde highlights too. There's just something about getting your hair done that makes you feel so much better. My next stop is the grocery store. I've only been eating one meal a day, mostly consisting of nothing but popcorn, crackers, cheese, or yogurt for the past several months, and it's time to start eating well again. I buy a ton of healthy food, and when I get home, I meal prep my lunch and dinner for the entire week.

Over the next couple of weeks, I get stronger and can now do my workouts all the way through to the end again. I gain back eleven pounds and finally get my hair done. I'm starting to feel happy again, and I'm actually enjoying some time to myself. I honestly don't miss Noah much, just the person he was at the beginning of our marriage. I did miss that person for a while.

The person I really miss is Jordan. That hasn't wavered one bit. I still love him and I want to see him.

I head to my regular Friday session with Nelly, and at the end, she says, "Kate, you look good. I was worried for a while, but the past few weeks I've seen a big change. I can tell you are back on track, and I'm so happy to see it."

"I feel good, I really do. I want to ask you about Jordan. I haven't seen him or spoken to him, I swear. But my feelings for him haven't changed at all. I miss him. I want to see him."

She leans back in her chair and says, "Well, you did everything I asked you to do. You worked on yourself and didn't give in to the temptation to call him or see him, and I know that had to be extremely difficult for you. If you feel ready to see him, then that's your decision. But, and this is a huge Kate, do not jump into a relationship with him. Talk to him. See where he stands and go from there. Slowly! And be prepared to find out that he might have moved on. There's always a chance that he has."

I tell her that I understand and that I will be careful. My time is up. My sessions are now two weeks apart, so I tell her I'll see her then.

When I get home, I stare at my phone and almost call Jordan about ten times. But then I have another idea. It's Friday and it's a little past noon. I touch up my makeup, fix my hair, spray on my perfume, and change into a new sundress I just bought.

At 1:50 I pull into the parking lot of the organic market, which I haven't been to for over six months. I park my car, but before I get out, I glance in my rearview mirror. I smile when, in the very last row, I see a familiar dark blue car…